The evening was definitely over

It helped, Margaret found, if she kept repeating it to herself. Aloud she said, "It was very pleasant, but it's time to say good-night."

"So it is." A slow grin lifted Dom's lips, and sudden panic caught her. "It isn't midnight yet, though, Cinderella." He reached out for her and she tried to step back.

He gathered her to him, lifted her easily free of the floor, and his flaxen head bent unhurriedly. His lips covered her mouth in a long kiss, starting the wild singing in her veins that she didn't want to hear again. She had to stop him somehow.

She kicked him. Hard. Driving her feet against his shins. "Go away and tame your wildcat well!" she shouted at him furiously. "You can't tame me that way!"

OTHER
Harlequin Romances
by SUE PETERS

Many of these titles are available at your local bookseller.

For a free catalogue listing all available Harlequin Romances, send your name and address to:

HARLEQUIN READER SERVICE,
M.P.O. Box 707, Niagara Falls, N.Y. 14302
Canadian address: Stratford, Ontario, Canada N5A 6W2

Claws of a Wildcat

by

SUE PETERS

Harlequin Books

TORONTO • LONDON • LOS ANGELES • AMSTERDAM
SYDNEY • HAMBURG • PARIS • STOCKHOLM • ATHENS • TOKYO

Original hardcover edition published in 1980
by Mills & Boon Limited

ISBN 0-373-02368-5

Harlequin edition published November 1980

CHAPTER ONE

'Men! They're one commodity I could do without!'

'He couldn't help getting his face cut,' Bill pointed out mildly.

'They were two grown men, fighting like a pair of silly schoolboys,' Margaret retorted scathingly. 'And as a result, we've both had an hour's unnecessary hard work we could well have done without. Like I could do without men, right now,' she reiterated feelingly.

'Not present company, I hope?' Bill Quinn perched his angular frame nonchalantly on a corner of the leather-topped desk and regarded her quizzically.

'Certainly not present company,' Margaret amended hastily. 'With the Chief skittering off down country, and leaving us short-handed, I can't do without you as well.'

'Nice to know you're wanted,' her white-coated companion grinned. 'But be fair,' he urged, 'the Chief's hardly on a pleasure cruise. I should think trying to squeeze money out of the powers that be, for a new wing here, is a mission designed to make him a patient in his own hospital by the time he returns,' he predicted gloomily.

'I know.' Margaret Warrender passed a hand across her forehead with a weary gesture and leaned back in the shabby hide chair that was built to take the bear-like bulk of Neil Venables, her absent Chief, and dwarfed her own slight figure so that she seemed lost in its well-worn depths.

'You're tired,' the young house surgeon eyed her narrowly. 'Being in charge while Neil's away doesn't usually bother you.'

'I know,' she confessed, feeling rather ashamed now of her sudden outburst. 'And under our normal workload, it wouldn't worry me now. It's just. . . .' Her voice trailed off.

'We've always had the losers of Saturday night free-for-alls in Casualty,' Bill pointed out philosophically.

'I know that, too, but these days it seems to be a never-ending stream,' Margaret protested. 'We're just not big enough to cope any longer.'

'Which is why the Chief's gone south with a begging bowl to get some more money to build an extension, and employ extra staff,' Bill repeated patiently.

'That won't help us now.' She was not to be appeased. 'It isn't as if it's all happened gradually,' she wailed despairingly.

'Like evolution, you mean?' her companion asked amusedly.

'Call it what you like,' she retorted crossly, 'the town has nearly doubled its population within the space of a few weeks, since the oil companies decided to come exploring in the area, and it feels as if we've been taken over by an invading horde. Why did they have to park their beastly oil rig just offshore of us?' she demanded peevishly.

'Because that's where they reckon they'll find the oil, I guess. It's exciting when you think about it,' Bill warmed to the subject. 'Who'd have thought our insignificant little patch of the globe would sport an oil well?' he asked.

'It doesn't, yet,' she retorted crushingly. 'From what I can gather, they're still prospecting, or whatever it is they do for oil,' she shrugged indifferently. She was not particularly interested in what they did, only in its effect on the beleagured Meldonmouth General Hospital.

'Future oil well, then,' Bill conceded.

'It's the present I'm worried about,' Margaret interrupted impatiently. 'The town's expanded to bursting point, and we simply haven't got the facilities or the staff to cope. And as as if that isn't enough,' she went on, her voice rising, 'before he went away Neil agreed that we'd provide an emergency back-up medical service to the oil rig—if required,' she emphasised, heavily sarcastic. 'How many pairs of hands do they think we've got?' she asked wrathfully. 'I'm beginning to feel like an octopus as it is!'

'That's only in case of a dire emergency,' Bill placated. 'Their own resident medical staff on the rig would cope in all but exceptional circumstances. I'd be interested to see over the rig hospital,' he added, 'it might be miniature, but from what Neil told me, they're remarkably well equipped. No expense spared, apparently,' he added wistfully.

'We haven't got an oil company sponsoring us,' Margaret retorted drily, 'so let's hope a dire emergency doesn't arise, at least until Neil can beg enough funds for an extension. The people from the rig and their families are proving about the last straw for the General as it is, without drawing staff away from the hospital to cope outside.'

'The oil men seem a fairly quiet lot on the whole,' Bill replied mildly, 'it's only when they change crews on the rig, they seem to celebrate.'

'They're no better and no worse than the locals,' Margaret acknowledged, 'it's just that they're doubling our workload on an already over-stretched Casualty Department, in what is, after all, little more than a cottage hospital. That man's face, tonight....' Despite her years of experience, she shuddered. 'He was one of the oil rig crew. I can't remember what he said he did. It sounded something like a roundabout,' she said vaguely.

'What's the matter with his face?' a cheerful voice asked her.

'Sue!' Margaret sat up and stared at the newcomer in surprise. 'What are you doing here at this time of the night? Therapists work civilised hours,' she added enviously.

'I came to pick up my fiancé.' Sue Marlow dropped a light kiss on Bill's wiry dark head. 'When he's on this shift, it's the only way I get to see him. Who'd marry a doctor?' she sighed.

'You're going to.' Bill reached out a possessive arm.

'Hey, watch what you're doing!' She neatly dodged his grasp. 'You'll spill the coffee.'

'Coffee? You angel!' The house surgeon grasped gratefully at her offering, and Sue laughed.

'It's all cupboard love, with the men.' She handed another cup to Margaret. 'Sister Casualty said you'd had a busy time tonight, and I guessed a hot drink wouldn't come amiss. Even if it is out of a plastic beaker,' she grimaced.

'It's nectar.' Margaret sipped her own with a relish she rarely accorded the outpourings of the mechanical drinks dispenser.

'What about the man you were talking about, when I came in? What happened to him?' Sue asked curiously.

'He got cut across the face and head by broken glass,' Margaret said briefly. 'I stopped counting after I'd put forty stitches in him.'

'One of his mates crowned him with a bottle, and it broke,' Bill explained succinctly. 'What a waste of good Scotch,' he mourned. 'Still, it had one beneficial effect, the whisky cleaned the cut as soon as it was done, there wasn't a germ to be seen by the time he got here.'

'With a cut like that, he was lucky to get here at all.'

'His mate brought him in. He wouldn't have made it, otherwise.'

'You mean the man who hit him?' Sue regarded him incredulously.

'He didn't mean to hit him so hard. He said it was an accident that the bottle broke,' Bill said seriously, 'and I believed him. Fortunately there's no permanent harm done, it missed his eyes.'

'What on earth were they fighting about?'

'A woman.' Bill leered at the brown-haired therapist. 'What else is there worth fighting over?' he said sententiously.

'Clot!' Sue cuffed him lightly, and wriggled into a comfortable position on his knee. 'You'll get into rare trouble if you're found cuddling me while you're on duty,' she said, with not very convincing severity.

'There probably won't be any more patients until the morning,' Bill murmured contentedly. 'The pubs closed an hour ago, and anything the homegoing tide was likely to wash in our direction has beached by now,' he said with the confidence of long experience.

'Like that man?'

'Like that man,' her fiancé agreed solemnly. 'What a waste of. . . .'

'Good Scotch,' Sue finished for him with a laugh. 'You're impossible!' she scolded.

They both were. Impossibly in love. Margaret eyed them with a stirring of something that in anyone else she might have suspected was envy. She wondered, not for the first time, how Sue could contemplate giving up a promising career for marriage. It was different for Bill. Men had the best of both worlds, she thought dispassionately, they could get married and still keep their careers. But now, as she looked at Sue snuggled cosily on Bill's knee, her wondering unexpectedly took another direction. Perhaps if . . . she pulled her thoughts to a halt, sharply.

'I *am* tired,' she told herself. 'Or else it's spring coming, or something.'

'I wish you wouldn't stick your stethoscope in that pocket,' Sue complained lazily, without bothering to move. 'It digs in.'

'Don't get too comfortable,' Margaret warned, and found herself taken off guard with a sigh. She did not envy Sue and Bill, why should she? Domesticity did not appeal to her, as it did to the therapist. She had not gone through all those years of training just to give it all up in order to wash dishes. Sue might think the sacrifice was worth it, but for herself—her career was the most important thing in her life. She had never questioned that. Until tonight. . . . So why did she sigh? She got to her feet abruptly.

'Bill's off duty as from now,' she consulted her watch ostentatiously. 'Take him away, Sue, his stint's finished for tonight.' For some reason she wanted, suddenly, to be left on her own, even though normally she welcomed the company of the cheerful young couple. But tonight she did not want to sit and watch them in each other's arms.

'I'll stay on for a bit if you like, just in case?' Bill offered, and sent her a keen look across the desk. 'Maggie's tired,' he stilled Sue's quick protest.

'I'm fine now I've had a sit down and some coffee,' Margaret refused him firmly. 'And don't call me Maggie,' she snapped. 'Besides, your stand-in's just arrived,' she covered her sharpness with a hasty explanation, as the unmistakable throaty exhaust of a sports car roared to a halt outside the windows, and burbled into silence even as she spoke.

'In that case, I'm pursuaded.' Bill Quinn yawned, stretched, and grasped the brown-haired Sue round her waist. 'See you tomorrow, Maggie,' he jibed with a grin.

'Oh, come on!' Sue raised her eyes ceilingwards, grimaced an apology at Margaret, and pulled the young house surgeon unresisting through the door. And left behind a strange feeling of emptiness. Margaret examined it curiously. The emptiness felt as if it was inside her, and had nothing to do with the now silent room. It was not as if something was missing. Rather, as if it had never been. Like a melody played too softly for the listener to quite catch, but haunting the senses nevertheless, making its presence felt even if the sound itself could not be heard. A glimpse of a rainbow, just as it fades....

The three empty plastic beakers littering the desk seemed somehow to symbolise the strangeness of her mood. They were frail, transient, throw-away things, empty. Slowly she reached out and picked them up one by one and stacked them tidily together, then dropped them into the waste basket. The cleaners would remove them when they started their early morning shift.

'Doctor Warrender?' A light tap sounded on the office door, and Bill Quinn's stand-in poked his head through.

'Yes? What is it?'

A surge of irritation went through her. The man was new to the hospital, and insufferably formal. Belatedly, she remembered she had snapped at Bill for being just the opposite.

'Perhaps he'll put it down to the colour of my hair, and not a nasty nature,' she thought remorsefully, and raked quick fingers through her close-cropped red-gold hair. She summoned up what she hoped was an encouraging smile, and wondered how she could manage it when she felt like literally dropping on her feet.

'There's someone called to collect a patient, and Sister won't let him go unless you give permission.'

The smile must have worked, because the newcomer came further into the room and returned it, albeit tentatively.

'I'll come.'

They had only warded one patient that evening, the man with the cut face. She followed her staff man towards the Casualty waiting room, and looked round.

'Who . . .?' She expected to see a woman, the woman Bill Quinn said the men had been fighting over. Instead,

'I understand you've got one of our roustabouts here.'

He turned with a lithe grace from where he had been standing by the window overlooking the concrete ambulance driveway. He had scorned the two rows of empty chairs, as if he found even the spacious waiting room confining, and opted instead for the wide expanse of glass as the nearest he could get to out-of-doors.

'He collected a cut face, or something,' he offered helpfully, as if he thought Margaret might not be able to identify the victim from his perfunctory explanation.

She scarcely heard what he said. His words hardly registered against the impact of the man himself. As he turned, she had to raise her eyes a full foot to take in a head of flaxen fairness, his hair looked almost white under the pitiless fluorescent lighting, the startling lightness of it accentuated by the dark mahogany tan of his face, and eyes the deepest blue she had ever seen. They regarded her with dawning impatience.

'I've come to collect a man with a cut face,' he insisted, and raised his voice, as if he thought she had not heard him the first time.

'Yes, I know. You said.' She found herself stammering. 'I can't release him, not tonight.'

What on earth was the matter with her? She was reacting like a gauche schoolgirl, she thought disgustedly, and fought down a feeling of almost physical shock that sent her tired senses reeling. No man had the right to look like this, she thought dazedly. He towered above her, all six feet plus of him, like a reincarnation of one of the gods of ancient Norse legend; incredibly tall, incredibly fair, and almost unbelievably handsome. She swallowed convulsively, and managed to find her voice.

'Come back tomorrow about eleven o'clock. He should be fit enough to be discharged by then.'

Automatically her eyes sought the plain, round face of the electric clock above the entrance doors. The hands said just after midnight. Perhaps that explained it, she thought, with a sudden hysterical desire to giggle. The strange witching hour, that was neither night nor morning, when footsteps made hollow echoes in the empty corridors, whose daytime bustle was peopled now only by shadows.

She *was* in a strange mood tonight! She almost wished she had risked Sue's displeasure and accepted Bill's offer to remain for a while. The house surgeon's cheerful matter-of-factness was the perfect antidote to the intrusion of fey thoughts, which never normally bothered her. Usually she was too busy to think about anything but immediate necessities. Near-exhaustion must have made her vulnerable.

'I can't come back at eleven o'clock tomorrow.' The impatience manifested itself in a quick spark of anger, and his voice hardened perceptibly. 'I've got something better to do than ride herd on a roustabout,' he told her bluntly, 'he'll have to come now, while I've got the helicopter available.'

'That's quite impossible.' Margaret's chin came up, and

her green eyes flashed fire, and the temper that went with her rich red-gold hair rose at the curtness of his tone. 'The man's injured.'

'From what I heard, it's his own fault,' he replied uncompromisingly.

'That's not my concern,' Margaret snapped. The man was impossible, she thought angrily—too sure of his own good looks, and expected other people to fall in with his every whim because of them, she diagnosed caustically. She felt too tired to be either generous, or just, tonight.

'He lost a lot of blood, and we had to give him a transfusion. And now he's sleeping it off,' she informed him coldly. 'Of course, if you want to carry him. . . .' Her voice bit.

'No, thanks,' he refused shortly. 'He's made his bed, let him lie on it,' he added callously. A slight grin tilted the corners of his well cut lips. 'I leave him in your tender, loving care.' The mocking inflection in his voice questioned whether she, personally, was capable of any of the three, but before she could find breath to retort, he turned on his heel and strode away, and only the swinging double doors told where he had been.

'Well! Of all the arrogant, conceited. . . .' Margaret expelled her breath in a furious hiss.

'You must admit he's got something to be conceited about.' Underneath Sister Casualty's efficient exterior beat an incurably romantic heart. 'Who is he, anyway?' she asked curiously.

'He must be one of the oil men,' Margaret answered her in a clipped voice. 'Certainly he's a stranger to the town, if you don't know him.' Her buxom companion was a great socialiser, and knew practically everyone in the small coastal town by name or sight, a fact which made her a mine of useful information to the medical staff on the backgrounds of their various patients.

'I wonder what he does?' Sister pursued interestedly.

'I couldn't care less,' Margaret retorted irately. 'It's what he is, not what he does, that's rattled me. He's. . . .'

'Arrogant and conceited. I heard you,' the older woman laughed. 'But perhaps he's got problems, too,' she appeased. As well as being a romantic, she was a born peacemaker, and Margaret smiled at her affectionately.

'Point taken,' she conceded, 'though I still don't like the man, for all his good looks.' She wrinkled her nose disgustedly. 'But if it's any help, he's probably a pilot,' she offered, and her eyes crinkled with amusement at the prick of instant interest on the other's face. 'He mentioned he'd got a helicopter here,' she enlarged obligingly. 'But no doubt you'll learn more from "cut face" in the morning, when he wakes up,' she predicted with a fair degree of accuracy. 'That is, if his head doesn't ache too much to talk.'

'The whisky bottle that hit him was a full one, he hadn't had time to celebrate,' Sister retorted with a dry practicality that drew a chuckle from Margaret in spite of her tiredness. 'But when I find out more, I'll let you know, if you like,' she offered shamelessly.

'I don't like. I'm not interested,' Margaret retorted, and gave a quick, vexed wriggle. 'I still feel ruffled all over,' she confessed.

'Go home and get some sleep,' Sister advised. 'You should have been off duty hours ago. Nothing else is likely to crop up tonight, now,' she followed Bill Quinn's reasoning. 'And you only live a few steps away, we can call you if necessary.'

The few steps was, in fact, ten minutes' brisk walk to the other end of the horseshoe-shaped harbour, but if she was wanted urgently she could be back at the hospital in under five with the help of the bicycle she kept for just such emergencies, and for her all too rare forays into the gently rounded Meldon Hills that sheltered the little town on its landward side.

She hung up her white overall and shrugged into her coat. In spite of the end-of-February cold, intensified by the late hour, she left it unbuttoned and swinging free. Her matching tweed skirt and Arran sweater were warm, and she thrust her hands deep into the pockets and lifted her face to the keen night air, welcoming its sharpness on her fine, flawless skin.

She stood for a few moments outside the swing doors, the ones through which the flaxen-haired stranger had so recently disappeared, and took a deep breath. The cold was invigorating, washing away some of her tiredness, and bringing back a measure of her accustomed calm. But for all its tonic properties she still felt strangely unsettled.

There was no reason for it that she could put her finger on. The only difference in the past week from her normally busy routine was her Chief's absence, which made it even busier. Perhaps the strain was beginning to tell. Perhaps. . . . Her feet lagged on the smooth, hard cobbles, her train of thought halting their progress, so that she turned across the narrow street and leaned her arms along the harbour wall, a dark line under the faint starlight from the cold, polished galaxy far above her head.

Could it be that tiredness was at last tearing down the barriers which, over the years, she had allowed her work to erect round her? Self-delusion was not something Margaret was prone to, and she gazed down at the dark water that she could hear better than she could see, lapping against the stone far below. Her work had become a barrier, she admitted to herself honestly, particularly since she had been promoted to second Neil as next in command at the General, the long hours and added responsibility had become a kind of armour, which imprisoned her as a person as much as it kept at bay the world outside. Was Margaret Warrender in danger of becoming lost inside the starched white coat of Doctor Warrender? she asked herself, in her unusual midnight mood of introspection.

She shivered, but whether it was from the trend of her own thoughts or the numbing coldness of the granite on which she leaned, she did not bother to ask herself. She knew she ought to go home. She needed rest, she had been on duty for fourteen strenuous hours, and she would be on duty again tomorrow, and every day after that until Neil Venables was able to return and take over his own work-load again on to his own broad shoulders.

But still she lingered, conscious of, but ignoring, the cold. Usually the peace of the converted fisherman's cottage which was her home exerted an irresistible pull at the end of a busy day. Its tastefully furnished rooms spoke eloqu-ently of her care. Furniture upholstered in handmade tapestry and delicately worked covers told of her love of embroidery, worked during the scarce, precious hours when she could sit in the window overlooking the harbour, and unwind from the stress of the day. But tonight she felt oddly reluctant to return to the silent, empty cottage.

'It's Bill's fault,' she told herself with a wry attempt at humour. Seeing Bill and Sue together tonight, young, eager, and very much in love. Not all that much younger than she was herself, but at the moment she felt immeasur-ably older than her twenty-eight years. She sighed, and pushed herself off the wall.

'If you don't get some sleep, you'll never reach twenty-nine,' she told herself sternly, and turned determinedly to-wards the dark huddle of cottages at the end of the harbour, only to pause again as the faint noise of an engine broke the night time silence. A late night reveller, perhaps? Unlikely, in Meldonmouth, there were no entertainments open, even on a Saturday night, later than eleven o'clock. She looked up. The sound came from the sky, not the road.

It did not take her long to locate it. Guided by the noise, her eyes soon picked up the pinprick of light, and the heli-copter that bore it, heading steadily out to sea, no doubt to the oil rig that stood offshore. She stood still and watched it until it disappeared from sight in the darkness, its light becoming indistinguishable among the background of bril-liant stars.

Then, and only then, when the noise died away in the

distance, and her straining eyes could no longer make out
the dark shape of the machine against the sky, she turned
and walked slowly in the direction of her cottage. And wondered, as she walked, why it was that her exhaustion-dazed
mind should still be able to print such a vivid picture of
the man who she felt certain must be at the controls of the
machine.

His mahogany face. His wavy, flaxen hair. And a pair of
the bluest eyes she had ever seen.

CHAPTER TWO

'COME back again at the end of the week and have the
stitches taken out.'

Sister Casualty's familiar words greeted Margaret as she
finished her ward rounds and made her way to her office
the next morning.

'Aw, I'll get here if I can. Depends on whether the
'copter's coming in or not, and what time,' a deep voice
drawled. 'If I can't get in, I'll keep 'em as souvenirs,' the
owner of the stitches announced cheerfully.

Cut face!

Margaret stared at him in surprise. Their half-uncon-
scious casualty of the previous night sat chatting to Bill
Quinn as if nothing had happened. He seemed as uncon-
cerned as he was unaffected by his ghastly adventure.

'He's fit enough to be discharged,' Bill stated unnecessarily as she walked towards them, and his eyes twinkled.

'I can see that.' Margaret could not hide her astonishment as their burly patient bounded to his feet with an
energy he could not possibly have assumed, and took her
hand in a hard, horny grip.

'Doc here says you tied me together last night,' he
boomed. 'I'm sure obliged.'

A crooked grin defied the criss-cross of mends on his face, and Margaret smiled, warmed by his rough gratitude.

'I expect your own M.O. on the oil rig will take the stitches out when they're ready,' she suggested, but added an automatic caution, 'Take care. Take things easy for a couple of days or so.'

'On an oil rig? You must be joking!' Bushy eyebrows rose in undisguised hilarity. 'No chance, lady, it's all go out there.' He forgave her ignorance with ribald humour. 'See you.' He took his leave with a laconic nod. 'Ready when you are, mister.' He spoke to someone over Margaret's shoulder, and with the same casual lack of ceremony he did not bother to wait for whoever it was. With an indifference to the hospital woodwork that Margaret did not know whether to feel indignant about or laugh at, he put his booted toe to the base of the swing doors, kicked a passage through for himself, and let them swing shut behind him without a backward glance, leaving the person he had spoken to to follow at his leisure.

Margaret started to turn. Perhaps that person might listen to her cautionary advice, even if their patient would not.

'Make him steady down for the next twenty-four hours,' she instructed, 'just until the shock's worn off. Or better still, leave him ashore for that length of time.'

'I don't intend to try and make him do anything of the sort,' a voice answered her crisply. 'And as for letting him remain ashore, that's out of the question.'

At the sound of his words Margaret felt as if her patient's shock had transmitted itself to her. She lifted her head. His eyes were even bluer than she remembered them. And the cold light of day did nothing at all to detract from his startling good looks.

'It's his own fault he got damaged,' the flaxen-haired man's tone got even crisper. 'If he does anything silly now, and suffers for it, he'll learn all the quicker not to get into fights.'

He was just as callous as she remembered, too. The

smouldering fires of last night's anger flared in her afresh, and she snapped,

'If you'd exercise more control over your men, it wouldn't have happened in the first place!'

'In the first place, he's not my man.' He aimed a level look at her, and she met it unflinchingly.

'You came back specially for him.'

'On the contrary,' he denied smoothly, 'I came ashore to suit my own convenience.' His indifference was almost insulting, but before she could think of a reply he went on, 'The fact that a roustabout from the rig spent the night in hospital, and needs a lift back, is purely coincidental. Now I'm here, I may as well give him a lift, it would be a waste of fuel to send for him specially.' Blue eyes clashed with flashing green ones, openly challenging her to fault his reasoning.

'Is that what he is? A roustabout?' Bill Quinn's interested enquiry diffused the silent antagonism that ran like an electric current between them, so strong that it seemed to Margaret as if she could almost hear the hiss of it, burning through her senses like a penetrating fire. 'It sounds more like a job around a ranch than on an oil rig,' the house surgeon pursued curiously.

'It probably covers a similar sphere of activity,' the flaxen-haired man volunteered his opinion, which had not been asked for, Margaret thought tartly. 'The roustabouts do general labouring on the rig. And as such,' his eyes swivelled to fix on Margaret, and she had the peculiar conviction that he was speaking to her alone, excluding Bill Quinn, 'as such they are indispensable. An oil rig carries no passengers.'

'Neither does a hospital,' she was stung to retort, but he ignored her remark as if she had not spoken, she thought furiously, and continued,

'If one man falls by the wayside, his duties have to be carried by someone else. Which is why the man you stitched up last night knows he can't have an extra twenty-four hours on shore to lark about in.' His lips closed on the end of his sentence with an almost audible snap.

'I'd hardly call what happened last night larking about,' Margaret began hotly.

'But in fact that's just what it was,' he insisted. 'It started as a joke.'

'As a joke, it misfired,' Bill butted in grimly. 'Pretty badly, too, from the state the man was in when he reached us. What on earth happened?'

'The rig staff do fourteen days about,' their informant explained patiently. 'A couple of weeks on the rig, a couple of weeks shore leave. The man you had in last night was on his way to the air-strip to pick up the helicopter ready to start his shift on the rig. He stopped off to have a drink with his opposite number coming on leave, and he was unwise enough to tell his oppo he had,' he paused slightly, 'looked after the other man's wife while he was ashore,' he finished significantly. The blue eyes bored into Margaret's, a stirring of sardonic amusement in their gentian depths. Watching her, to see what her reaction would be to his words.

If he's trying to shock me, that's misfired as well, she thought with satisfaction. He ought to have more sense than to think he could shock a doctor. Her chin came up.

'And had he?' she asked deliberately. 'Looked after her, I mean?' She underlined her comprehension of what he had implied, but instead of her own bluntness disconcerting him, as she meant it to, the laughter in his eyes grew until it creased the corners in a myriad tiny lines.

'As a matter of fact—no,' he let the laughter show, and Margaret compressed her lips. 'I told you, it was only meant as a joke. Unfortunately the other man took him seriously, and reacted in the only way that presented itself at the time.'

'By wasting a whole bottle of perfectly good Scotch.' Bill Quinn could not find it in his heart to forgive the wielder of the bottle for such wanton destruction.

'The rig men value their women,' was the dry reply, and Margaret's eyes snapped.

'Even above a bottle of whisky?' she enquired stiffly. She noticed he said 'women', not 'wives', which showed his own opinion of the opposite sex, and she bridled resentfully.

'Just about,' his look openly taunted her, sensing her hostility, and deriving uncaring amusement from it. Prickles of anger ran up her spine at his attitude. 'They must do,' he shrugged indifferently, 'they bring them along when we move locations, which means a pretty unsettled existence for the women and children. And then the men only get to see them for a fortnight at a time.'

'If they don't like the way they live, why don't they get a nine-to-five job, then they could go home at night and bed their wives, or whatever, and everybody would be happy,' she flared—and promptly went scarlet to the roots of her hair. She felt, rather than saw, Bill's stare of undisguised astonishment, and felt hot all over at what he must be thinking. She did not trust herself to look at him. Instead she grasped desperately at her rapidly slipping composure, and glared at the flaxen-haired stranger.

'I'll suggest it, to the two men who were fighting.' Strong white teeth gleamed in a grin as he tossed back her snub, and widened into silent laughter at her treacherous, heightened colour. 'I'm sure they'll appreciate your advice—doctor.'

'You could heed it yourself.'

She did not know what made her say it. Some imp inside her, and totally out of her control, and of whose existence she had never before been aware, seemed to goad her on, stampeding her over the edge of good manners in a way that was totally uncharacteristic, but she resolutely thrust down any compunction she might feel at her own behaviour. The man deserved it, she told herself angrily.

'I travel alone.' Once again she had the uncanny feeling that his words were meant to hold some significance for her, that they were directed at her like a barb, intended to find its mark. 'I can't be bothered with encumbrances, however attractive.'

His eyes flicked over her for what seemed an endless minute, then with a curt nod to Bill he was gone, with the same lithe, easy stride that took him through the swing doors and out of her sight the night before, they swallowed him now, and left her, once more, fighting for composure, and undoubtedly the loser in this second battle of wills, rather than words, that had just passed between them. She took a deep breath and willed herself to stand perfectly still until she had counted up to ten. She reached five when Bill gave vent to a low whistle.

'Phew!' He sent a awestruck look in her direction. 'Our shy little Maggie's got claws when she needs them!'

'How did you . . .?' She bit her lip, and stopped. Bill was a house surgeon, not a psychiatrist. How had he managed to guess at the inherent shyness that lay deep within her sensitive nature, and she confidently believed until now was well and truly masked by the calm professionalism for which she was renowned at the General.

'You've got a chink in your armour, Maggie,' he enlightened her softly, affectionately, and she stared at him in stunned consternation.

How did he know she wore armour? She had only discovered it last night for herself.

'You shouldn't own red hair, and the fine skin that goes with it,' Bill chided her kindly. 'It acts just like a barometer to your feelings.'

'I feel as if the mercury is about to boil over the top.' Margaret expelled a long breath, and managed a rather forced laugh. 'I hope to goodness we're never called on to back up the medical services on the oil rig, if it means meeting that man again,' she ejaculated. 'That's twice he's been here, and so far as I'm concerned, it's twice too often.'

'Hmmm.' Bill's eyes held a twinkle. 'You did rather give the impression that you'd enjoy sticking a hypodermic in him,' he understated. 'Good and deep, where it hurts most,' he chuckled.

'I felt strongly tempted last night,' she confessed, her mood lightening a little under his friendly teasing.

'So Sister told me.'

'Sister's an incurable gossip.'

'Save your comments,' Bill warned, 'she's just bringing us some customers. If it's the lady who needs a soothing hand, allow me the privilege,' he begged shamelessly. 'She's lovely.'

'I agree.' The young Jamaican girl, about Sue's age, who followed Sister's buxom figure in their direction looked as if she had stepped straight from a painting, rather than from real life. She carried a child, a boy of nearly two, and it flashed across Margaret's mind that they would make a perfect picture of the Madonna and Child, except for the strained look of worry in the mother's liquid dark eyes, and the child's restless twisting in her arms, that spoke of pain. The father hovered over them protectively, his ebony hands fumbling a battered teddy bear with which he had obviously been trying to comfort the baby.

'We thought it was a tooth at first, but it seems to be more in the region of his ear than his gums.' The man spoke in an educated voice, with the resonant timbre from a deep-barrelled chest, denoting the likelihood of a fine singing voice and Margaret smiled reassuringly at the mother.

'Let me look at him.' She sat down and motioned the anxious parents to do the same.

'I'll give him a lift on to your lap,' Bill offered helpfully, and held out his hands, and the dismay on his face was comical when the baby let out a lusty yell.

'He doesn't like the look of you,' Margaret could not resist a chuckle.

'I'm sorry,' the mother was apologetic. She had a sweet, husky voice, and Margaret felt an instant attraction towards her. 'I don't think he's forgiven any of us yet for his immunisation jabs.'

'Let me try.' Margaret held out her hand for the toy. 'I'll borrow his teddy,' she said clearly, and was rewarded by a wary look. 'Teddy?' she enquired softly, and the toddler sat up with a wide-eyed stare, and to her surprise he held out chubby arms towards her, as if he expected to be picked up.

'That's his name too—Teddy, I mean,' the father said, low key, and Margaret flashed him a grateful look. The baby was lucky in his choice of parents.

'Let's shuffle a bit closer to one another,' she suggested to the mother, 'he might change laps without any fuss if we do.'

The ploy worked. Within a minute the small, warm body cuddled against her, grasping for the toy, and she shot Bill a triumphant glance, and almost laughed aloud at his disgusted expression. Then she hurriedly put out protective arms as the baby heaved himself to his feet on her lap. He smelt sweetly of fresh clothes and baby powder, and seemed ready enough to respond to her encouraging murmurs.

'Ouch!' They changed to a groan of agony as two small brown hands reached up and with unpredictable speed grabbed fistfuls of her curls.

'Teddy, don't! Loose, darling—oh Lex, do something, quick!' the mother implored her husband.

'Leave him, I'll cope,' Margaret managed to gasp. She wrapped hasty arms right round the toddler for safety sake, and tickled his ribs with the speed of desperation. To her relief that worked, too. He gave a squeal and a wriggle, and her smarting head was free.

'I'm so sorry. I don't think he's ever seen red hair before.' Worry and laughter struggled for supremacy on the father's face, and Margaret laughed too, putting him at ease.

'At least he's discovered it doesn't burn,' she retorted ruefully.

'Joy? What are you two doing here? What's the matter with Teddy?' Sue Marlow hurried across the polished Casualty floor. 'He's not ill, is he?' she cried anxiously, and dropped into the chair next to Margaret.

'He's got earache, and it seems to be getting worse.' The mother's face lit up in welcome as the therapist appeared, and she spoke as if she and Sue knew one another well. 'Lex and I got worried.'

'I should think so, poor wee soul!' Sue looked as concerned as the parents.

'I want to have a look without upsetting him if I can help it,' Margaret murmured to her.

'Which ear is it?' Sue responded instantly.

'The right one.'

'Come on, Teddy, let's play pussycats.' She promptly laid her own head on the edge of Margaret's knee, and to her surprise the baby stretched full length on her lap, closed his eyes, and went limp—with his tiny ear in just the right position for her to investigate. She did not waste time in asking questions. She held out her hand, and blessed Bill's quick response. The instrument she wanted appeared in her fingers, and with its aid the cause of the trouble was a mystery no longer. Deftly she exchanged the lighted instrument for a pair of long, slender forceps, and after a quick manipulation, and another close look to satisfy herself that all was well, she told Sue gratefully,

'You two can wake up now, here's the cause of the trouble.'

The therapist raised her head and took the forceps from her hand.

'It looks like one of those miniature plastic toys you get in Christmas crackers,' she frowned at the foreign body which Margaret had removed from the baby's ear.

'The little girl next door!' the mother exclaimed, relief and enlightenment chasing each other across her mobile features. 'She came in to show Teddy her birthday presents just after breakfast this morning. There was a cracker among them, I remember.'

'And he pushed this thing in his ear, to see what it felt like,' Margaret finished for her resignedly. 'They all do the same, at one time or another. It's lucky you happened to be along,' she thanked Sue feelingly.

'We've played pussycats before,' Sue explained her actions with a laugh. 'Teddy's seen my mother's old tabby, which does nothing but stretch out in front of the fire and sleep, and I reckon he thinks that all cats are alike. Wake up, poppet,' she gathered the toddler into her arms, 'let's get your poor mum and dad a cup of tea or something, they can probably do with a reviver,' she offered sympathetically.

'Come into my office and have it,' Margaret invited impulsively, 'we're due for our own break about now.'

'If we're not being a nuisance?'

'We'll be glad of your company,' Bill Quinn seconded the invitation hospitably. 'Sunday morning is always a quiet time in here.'

'We were going to church, and we landed here instead,' the mother told Sue ruefully.

'Never mind,' she consoled, 'you've settled Teddy's problem, and you've met my fiancé as well—I've been trying to bring him to see you for ages, only he never seems to be off duty these days.'

'I can't very well barge into a night school class for embroidery, can I?' Bill protested. 'It's hardly in my line.'

'I didn't mean come to the class, you goose,' Sue laughed, and turned to Margaret. 'Joy teaches us the finer points of embroidery at night school. I told you about the class. You ought to join us,' she urged. 'Margaret loves embroidery as much as I do,' she explained to Teddy's mother, 'but the trouble with doctors is they always seem to be on duty. It would do you good to get out for an evening, for a change,' she turned a severe look on Margaret.

'When Neil comes back, I might manage an evening occasionally. I'd like to, very much,' she discovered.

Whether it was the lingering remains of her restless mood of the night before, or the instant liking she felt for the Jamaican couple, or a mixture of both, Margaret did not question. She only knew she felt an irresistible urge to be herself for once, to break out of the armour and spread her wings like a butterfly emerging from the confinement of its chrysalis.

'Why not make a start tonight, and come and have supper with us?' Teddy's mother invited, and Margaret had the pleasant, warm feeling that her own liking was reciprocated. 'If things are quiet here, you may not get such a good opportunity again for a while. Come early,' she told Sue, 'you know where we live. And bring your fiancé, and Doctor—er——' she hesitated.

'Call me Margaret,' she begged impulsively.

'It makes it easier if we're on first name terms,' the other woman smiled. 'Can you and Bill both be off duty together?'

'Yes, we've got stand-ins for this evening, as it's the quietest night of the week,' Bill routed any lingering doubts that Margaret might have had. 'Provided we leave a message where we can be found in an emergency.'

'Have our address and telephone number.' Lex pulled a leather-covered notebook from his pocket and printed across it, then handed the sheet to Bill.

'Come about seven,' Joy suggested. 'By that time I'll have got this young man into bed,' she took her small son back from the reluctant Sue, 'and we can enjoy the evening in peace. The men will have one another to talk to about—whatever men do talk about.'

'Cricket,' said Lex.

'Soccer,' said Bill.

'Or argue about the merits of their respective sports,' Joy laughed, 'and we can enjoy ourselves with the embroidery.'

'You must love it, to be able to teach it as well.'

'I was teaching before I met Lex,' Joy told them. 'General teaching, at first, and then I specialised. It's a practical sort of hobby for me as well,' she added. 'With Lex away from home half of each month, I don't get much opportunity to indulge in cooking, and embroidery is easily packed, and light in weight when we have to move on. And taking a night school class is a quick way of making friends. That can be useful, too, when your husband's a semi-nomad,' she added rather wistfully.

It was only when she was dressing, preparatory to going out that evening, that a faint warning bell rang somewhere at the back of Margaret's mind. Her hand paused in the act of wielding her hairbrush, and she regarded her reflection in the mirror thoughtfully.

Why should Joy's words suddenly come back to her with such unexpected force?

'With Lex away from home half of each month. . . .'

For some reason she could not put her finger on, they seemed vaguely familiar, as if they might hold a special significance. But whatever it was, eluded her, and with a gesture of dismissal she put the faint, niggling question out of her mind, replaced her brush on her dressing table tray, and continued with the task of dressing for the evening.

CHAPTER THREE

'My word!' Bill Quinn's eyes held an appreciative gleam when he picked her up just before seven o'clock. 'Maggie in mufti puts Doctor Warrender in the shade,' he teased, and bowed her into his all purpose runabout beside Sue with exaggerated gallantry.

'Quell him, Sue.' Margaret settled herself in beside the other girl with a smile. 'And don't call me Maggie,' she scolded automatically, but it was doubtful if Bill heard her. He shut the door with a cheerful bang and went whistling round to the driver's seat.

'I don't think I could quell him tonight,' Sue laughed. 'He's like a child going to a party. And all because he's been asked out to supper. You know,' she turned to Margaret, and her face became serious, 'the Chief really will have to do something about getting extra staff, whether the hospital can afford it or not. It's weeks since Bill's had a day off, and it's been the same for you. Worse for you,' she amended truthfully, 'you've had to shoulder the extra responsibility while Neil's been away, as well.'

'I know how Bill feels,' Margaret admitted. She almost felt like whistling herself. Even the luxury of getting dressed up in something pretty and feminine, instead of her practical working garb, was something to be savoured and lingered over.

'You did say wear something informal?' She eyed Bill's business suit, and Sue's mink-coloured corded velvet pinafore style and dainty blouse with relief. Her own green wool dress, with its softly pleated collar that rose high at the back in the suggestion of a ruff, and made a perfect frame for her delicately boned face and striking colouring, would not be out of place. The discreetly draped bodice accentuated the softly rounded outline of her dainty figure, and the skirt flowed across her slender hips and swirled below her knees in the new, longer length which she liked so much, and which felt so strange after her much shorter, practical everyday garb of sweater and skirt and white hospital coat. Her only adornments were a silver rope around the throat of the dress to match the silver clasp at the belt, and the platinum watch, which had been her parents' gift, and which she was rarely without.

'It's easier for Joy and Lex if we do,' Sue responded. 'Most of their stuff's still either in store or in transit until they find out whether they're likely to settle down for a while, or have to move on again.'

Once more the elusive question reared at the back of Margaret's mind, bringing with it the same faint unease that had disturbed her while she was dressing.

'Turn right, here,' Sue leaned forward in her seat to direct Bill, and broke across her train of thought. 'It's the detached house on the right. They were lucky,' she explained, 'the man who owns it had to go abroad for a couple of years, and Lex was able to rent it, with the option to purchase if they have to stay.'

There it was again. That faint, half familiar comment, that stubbornly refused to be identified.

'It isn't often I get the opportunity to escort two gorgeous girls.' Bill was only half joking as he helped them out of the car, and Margaret's morale lifted a little. Now they were here, she felt oddly nervous.

'It's high time I went out more, no matter how busy I am,' she thought, aghast at her own reaction to the unexpected outing. Wearing the armour of her work had left her—the individual inside it—curiously vulnerable. For so long—far too long, she realised with dismay—her contact with other people had been confined to patients and colleagues, and on this, her first evening out in ages, going to people she felt immediately drawn to as soon as they met, she felt unsure of herself, so that she was glad that Bill and Sue were with her, though she could not imagine why she should need support on her visit to Joy and Lex; they seemed the friendliest couple imaginable.

'Take no notice of the chaos,' their hostess greeted them cheerfully, 'we're only half installed, yet.'

'We're rather a crowd, to descend on you like this before you're even moved in properly,' Margaret said guiltily.

'Nonsense!' Joy took her cream wool cape, and stroked it with appreciative fingers. 'Mmm, this is nice.' She herself was dressed in a deep amber wool two-piece, which set off her dusky skin and beautiful figure to perfection. 'We've invited someone else along, as well,' she smiled. 'He'll balance the numbers, and I'm sure you'll like him. He's a friend of Lex's. Their stints coincide on the rig, which is rather nice, because it means they're both on shore leave together.'

'I didn't know Lex was an oil man?'

The warning bell clamoured loudly in Margaret's mind, insisting on being heard. Lex and Joy were newcomers to Meldonmouth, she knew, but it had not occurred to her to wonder what Lex did for a living. Nowadays, so many people followed their calling from one end of the earth to the other, so that the world's professional population had to a large extent become what Joy had described her husband as—semi-nomads, in what was an accepted modern way of life.

'Come and meet your partner for the evening.' Lex's warm, all-embracing smile would have put even the shyest person at ease, she thought gratefully, as he ushered her into the room, where he turned her with his hand under her elbow to meet his friend.

'Dom, come and meet Doctor Warrender—Margaret to us,' he smiled. 'This is Dominic Orr, Margaret—Dom for short.'

The alarm bell gave a final violent clang, and went still. It had done its best, but she had not listened. Or, to be more precise, she had failed to interpret the message it tried so hard to convey.

'We've already met.' Somehow she managed to respond, but her voice sounded faint, even in her own ears.

'But we hadn't been introduced.' Flaxen hair, brushed back uncompromisingly close to his head, gleamed palely in the lamplight, and gentian blue eyes held her trapped. His hand came out and gripped her fingers in a hard clasp. 'Doctor Warrender was on duty when I collected the roustabout who'd been in a fight,' he told Lex.

'She's off duty now, and so is Bill,' Joy said firmly. 'So it's first names only, while they're here,' she dispelled any attempt at formality. 'We invited them out to give them a break from work.' And because she and her husband liked them, her smile added warmingly. 'Come on, Lex,' she stirred him to his duties, 'see to the drinks while I go and have a look at the supper.'

'How d'you do—Margaret?'

Suddenly they were alone together, left facing one another in a corner of the room while the others chatted round them a few yards distance that might have been a thousand miles.

He rolled her name round his tongue like a caress, softly savouring the sound of it. Mocking it? She could not tell. She caught her breath as the triple cadences fell from his lips, and wished desperately he would loose her hand, so that she could join the others and lose herself in their gay chatter. Dominic Orr had the power to divest her of her armour, and she resented it.

She did not feel like a doctor any longer. In his presence she felt all woman. She tried in vain to gather together the remnants of her professional control. As Doctor Warrender, she was accustomed to dealing with all kinds of emergencies at a moment's notice, without disturbing her outward calm. But this was one emergency over which she seemed to have no control, and the feeling of helplessness rankled. The sheer male magnetism of the man reached out to her, pierced right through her armour, and touched the vulnerable woman inside, stirring a response from deep within her of which she felt suddenly, breathlessly afraid.

'Can I go up and see Teddy before supper?' Sue asked eagerly, and Joy smiled her permission.

'He refused to go to sleep until you'd been.'

'He didn't quite make it,' Sue reported, rejoining them a few minutes later. 'He's sound asleep, he didn't even rouse when I kissed him.'

'He's had an adventurous day,' Lex said ruefully. 'And given us one, too. We told Dom how you rescued him from the consequences,' he handed Margaret a glass of fine, dry sherry. 'Dom's Teddy's godfather,' he explained.

'Anyone who rescues my godson deserves my consideration.'

Why did the faint emphasis he put on his words have the power to flick her like a whip? She remembered his caustic rejoiner to her own taunt, when they were both at the hospital.

'I travel alone . . . I can't be bothered with encumbrances —however attractive.'

Perhaps now and then, when he felt inclined, she thought sarcastically, he might come across a possible encumbrance whom he thought deserved his consideration. 'Well, he needn't consider me,' she told herself indignantly, and wished she did not have to sit beside him at the supper table. Wished, indeed, that Joy and Lex had not gone to the trouble to invite him on her behalf in the first place, as she felt sure the friendly couple had, simply so that she might not feel the odd one out at the party. She would have been more than content with the company of her host and hostess, and Bill and Sue. She could have relaxed, with them. As it was, seated round the circular supper table, that was large enough to give ample room and yet small enough to encourage a cosy, intimate feel among the party, she felt anything but relaxed.

By means of Joy sitting between their two male guests, and Lex between the two women, the party evened out nicely. Lex had travelled widely, and was an excellent raconteur, and Bill's eager interest in the oil exploration that had wrought such a sudden change in the small coastal town kept the conversation flowing over the beautifully cooked meal that told Margaret her hostess's talents were not confined to embroidery.

If it had not been for the presence of Dominic on her left-hand side, she would have been able to forget herself, and join in the lighthearted exchange of conversation and banter that flowed with the effortless ease of people who are genuinely enjoying one another's company.

'Once an oil man, always an oil man.' Joy lifted resigned hands to the ceiling. 'They're worse than explorers, once the bug bites them,' she exclaimed, 'always off to see what's on the other side of the hill.'

'More like gold prospectors,' Dom capped her thinking with a smile. 'After all, it's called black gold.'

'I do believe oil runs in the veins of these two,' Joy complained. 'When I think they could both have had nice stable careers. Lex's father did everything he could to persuade him to go into the family practice, and Dom could have had a nice peaceful university career.'

'University?'

Margaret gave her dinner partner a surprised look. She could not imagine Dominic Orr being content to pursue the career of a university professor, however interesting. There was an aura of dynamic force about him, leashed now, it was true, in deference to his sourroundings and his companions, controlled by an implacable self-discipline that Margaret sensed was an integral part of the man. But such a force, a fusion of high quality mental and physical alertness, would demand an outlet and refuse to be denied. Not for him the restrictions of the academic world.

'I thought you were a pilot?'

She had not meant to show curiosity. The words seemed to come of their own accord. Ruefully she remembered Sister Casualty's offer, 'When I find out more, I'll let you know, if you like.' And her own blunt refusal, which she wished, too late, she could reverse.

'Dom isn't a pilot.' Joy looked surprised. 'Oh, I see, he was using the helicopter when he came to pick up the roustabout. No wonder you thought....'

'Dom and I both pilot the Chinook,' Lex took up the explanation. 'We both qualified as pilots, and divers. There was no need really, but in our trade you never know quite what's going to crop up, and versatility can sometimes get you out of—er—a difficulty,' he shot a wary glance at his wife.

'Could save your life, you mean, when things get rough,' Joy retorted. 'As they frequently do on an oil rig, so don't try to pull the wool over my eyes,' she told her husband severely. 'You should know better by now.' She turned to Margaret. 'You'd think the sheer awfulness of the places where they go in search of oil would deter them, but it only seems to make them all the keener.' She had no illusions, and showed it. 'Deserts; ice caps; hurricane belts, they always seem to choose the places where the climate is at its very worst. Fancy leaving all that sunshine back home in Jamaica—I must be mad!' she exclaimed. But the look she directed at her husband told him she was happy, and intercepting it, Margaret once again felt a strange restlessness stir inside her. Joy and Lex were lucky in one another. If I ever get married, Margaret thought suddenly, I hope I'm as lucky as they are. But she was married to her profession. Her work was enough. It gave her contentment, fulfilment. With an effort, she dragged her mind back to what her hostess was saying.

'I suppose men are built that way, and it's no good trying to change them,' Joy accepted male eccentricities with a tolerant philosophy. 'Dom's a geologist,' she corrected Margaret's wrong impression. 'And Lex is the drilling engineer in charge of operations on the rig.'

'That's what makes us such a good team,' Dom commented from beside her, and Margaret slanted a quick glance of dislike in his direction. He would think of himself as good in whatever he undertook, she thought bitingly. It was typical of the man's arrogance.

'I drill up the samples and Dom checks them out for hydrocarbons,' Lex over-simplified their expertise. 'That tells Dom whether we're on the right track or not.'

'And if you're not?' Bill questioned.

'Then we plug the well, and try our luck somewhere else.'

'It's hardly a matter of luck,' came from Dom drily. 'You make it sound as if we simply toss for it, then tell you to start drilling where the coin comes down.'

'That's what it seems like you geologists do, sometimes,' Lex grumbled goodhumouredly.

'Take no notice of these two,' Joy begged her guests. 'They're for ever arguing. I think that's why Lex didn't follow his father and become a dentist, his patients wouldn't have been able to argue back.'

'I'm doing much the same sort of job now, drilling on the rig,' Lex pointed out laughingly, 'only I have to drill bigger holes.'

'You haven't gone deep enough with this one yet.' Dom's voice was suddenly serious.

'We're down to nearly five thousand feet.' Lex's face too had lost its smile. 'And you say none of the samples so far have come up with any signs of hydrocarbons,' he reminded the geologist quietly.

'They will,' Dom insisted. He leaned forward over the table, his dessert spoon dangling unheeded in his hand, the dish for which it was intended likewise ignored. 'They've got to. The seismic survey charts only confirm what I already know. There's an anticline under that basin, and it holds oil,' he stated adamantly. 'A lot of oil.'

'Hardy and Gibbons don't agree with you,' Lex replied evenly.

'Hardy and Gibbons are two top geologists—but in this case, they're wrong.'

Her flaxen-haired partner evidently entertained no doubts about his own rightness, thought Margaret with a flash of irritation.

'I hope so, for your sake.' Lex's face was suddenly troubled. 'You're taking on two of the topmost men in your own profession, as well as the main Board of Directors,' he warned.

'Because I know I'm right.'

'You've been right before, that's why the Board let you have your own way on a two against one vote,' their host conceded. 'You've got a sixth sense about oil.'

'There's no sixth sense about it,' Dom argued forcefully. 'It's purely a matter of logical deduction.'

'Logical deduction told two geologists a lot older than you are that we ought to start drilling miles away in the other direction,' his friend pointed out drily.

'If I'm wrong, I'll admit it, and we'll move out.'

How uncharacteristic! Margaret thought, with a sudden

flash of humour. She could not imagine Dominic Orr ever admitting to being in the wrong about anything.

'If you're wrong, *you* might have to move out,' Lex cautioned him seriously. 'Neither Hardy nor Gibbons will readily forgive you for making them back down. Your career could be at stake over this, Dom. The Board have spent a fortune on letting you have your own way, and if you can't produce results. . . .' His voice tailed off unhappily.

'They'll get their fortune back when the well starts producing,' the geologist stated confidently.

Margaret eyed him covertly. The supper table, with its snowy cloth and hospitable board; his supper companions; the warm, softly lighted room; all were invisible to the man by her side, she realised with a flash of insight. Dom was totally absorbed in the cut and thrust of his discussion with Lex, no longer host and guest but fellow specialists, sharpening rapier-keen minds on the steel of their joint interest.

She turned and looked more fully at the man by her side, no longer afraid that he might notice her watching him. His lean brown face was tense, his blue eyes blazed with the force of his conviction, trying to convince his friend. They looked straight past her, not seeing her, and inexplicably a feeling of cold descended on her, a mantle of depression that dropped like a grey cloud across the evening to which she had looked forward so eagerly.

Dom was no longer even in the room with them, she thought. Mentally, he was back on the oil rig, battling with the difficulties and dangers at which Joy had hinted; responding to the challenge that the high spirit of adventure within him demanded he should meet and overcome. A man among a world of men. A world in which women—encumbrances—had no part, she remembered with a flash of unexpected bitterness.

Yet that could apply equally well to herself, so why should she feel bitter? Her own innate sense of fairness made her regard herself, and her own career, with the same clear vision which she turned on the geologist, and his. Until twenty-four hours ago she had been totally immersed in her work to the exclusion of almost everything else. Certainly to the exclusion of marriage. The world of the hospital, and the interest and satisfaction she found there, had made everything else seem trivial by comparison. Until last night, when sheer exhaustion tore aside the barriers. She shivered, although the room was warm. She felt defenceless without the barriers—exposed, though to what she could not tell.

She might have succeeded in re-erecting them, except for this unexpected meeting with Dominic Orr. On her own ground, in the known, safe world of the hospital, she felt she could cope with him, if only just. But meeting him socially, unexpectedly, as her partner at an intimate supper party, with the symbol of her armour—her white starched coat—left behind along with the familiar environment, she felt out of her depth, and the flaxen-haired geologist intruded across the wreckage of her defences in a way that disturbed and frightened her.

'Isn't the well you're working on producing oil yet?' Bill enquired naïvely.

'Give us time!' Lex expostulated. 'We're drilling a wildcat. . . .'

'A—what?' Bill's eyebrows rose in comical astonishment.

'A wildcat—an exploratory well,' Lex explained. 'We take the rig out to where we think the oil lies. . . .'

'You're right over where the oil *is*,' Dom interpolated, and his voice had the inflexible quality of steel.

'That's still to be proved.' Lex's retort had a ring of challenge in it, and Margaret rejoiced to hear it. At least Dom did not get all his own way, she thought with satisfaction. Dominic? Dominate would have been a more appropriate description of the man.

'Just keep your team drilling, I'll give you all the proof you need, soon enough,' he said confidently.

'We'll go another thousand feet or so,' Lex conceded. 'If

you haven't come up with any signs of hydrocarbons by then....' He paused significantly, and an air of almost unbearable tension cut across the easy atmosphere of the supper table.

Lex is only doing this for Dom because of their friendship, Margaret thought intuitively. If it had not been for that, the engineer would have lent his weight on the side of the other two geologists—she could not remember their names—and taken the rig miles further on. Fervently she wished Lex had done so. If only he had, the problems at the hospital would never have arisen. And her own path need never have crossed with that of Dominic Orr.

'And what if your wildcat proves intractable?' Bill had a happy knack of ignoring tensions, and did so now.

'Then I shall tame it,' Dom stated softly, into the sudden silence that followed the house surgeon's question.

And although he spoke to Bill, his eyes, Margaret realised with a sharp, tingling awareness, his eyes were fixed on her.

CHAPTER FOUR

'BRING your coffee over to the fire, and come and have a look at my embroidery.'

Joy released her. Her gay voice broke through Margaret's daze, and with an almost physical effort she dragged her eyes away from the hypnotic pull of Dom's startling blue. Her breath came swiftly, as if the effort had been as much as she could manage. She got to her feet, shaken by the encounter, and her heart kept pace with her breath. The thud of her pulses in her ears sounded so loud that it felt as if the others must hear it too.

The blazing intensity of his brief stare held her like a magnet. It stripped aside the last frail remnants of her already shaky barriers, and bared the innermost secrets of her thoughts, while reserving his own; the blue light in his eyes was too bright for her to penetrate, dazzling her, so that she could not read what lay behind it.

She stumbled to her feet, her normal surefooted agility giving away to trembling clumsiness, and he put out both his hands to steady her. With a quick, sure grasp he caught her tilting chair in one and herself with the other, gripping her wrist with fingers of steel. Their touch seared through her flesh so that it felt as if when he removed them there would be burn marks for ever imprinted where they lay. The shock of their contact ran through her like an electric current, jolting her senses back to alertness again, even while it took away the remainder of her breath.

'Leave your coffee, I'll carry it for you.'

There was no escape. Instead of remaining at the table with the other men, Dom picked up her coffee cup and came with her to the fire, and Bill and Lex followed them.

'I didn't think you were interested in embroidery?' Sue's protest was only halfhearted, and instead of seeking a chair of her own to sit on, she appropriated Bill's knee as if she had grown there.

'I want to see what the work of a professional looks like,' Bill grinned, and drew her contentedly in to a more comfortable position on his lap.

Margaret hesistated. A three-seater settee was the nearest to the chair Bill and Sue occupied. But if she sat on the end closest to them, Dom might take the middle seat next to her. It would be the natural thing for him to do, for he still balanced her coffee cup in his hand.

She half turned to take it, to circumvent any move he might make to sit beside her; perhaps to free him from any slight obligation the situation might force on him to seek a seat beside her. She could not imagine Dom would feel himself bound by social obligations, she thought wryly. If they did not suit him he would be more likely to ignore them. To hold a man like Dominic Orr, she sensed the obligation would have to be of a much deeper nature, and be regarded by him, not by others, as important.

'You sit on one end of the settee and I'll sit on the other, and we can spread the embroidery on the cushion between us.'

Once again Joy rescued her. She dropped into the seat next to Bill's chair, and with a sense of relief Margaret subsided into the deep, comfortable cushions at the other end. As soon as she was settled a hand reached down and presented her with her coffee cup, and she took it from him and looked up, a murmur of thanks on her lips. It came out calm, polite, indifferent, her poise restored. She raised her cup to her lips, prepared to enjoy herself now she was freed from the concern of his close proximity—and almost choked on the hot liquid as Dom reached out and pulled up a high-seated easy chair and positioned himself right against her side at the end of the settee. His chair was higher than her own seat, and he seemed to loom over her, his arm resting on the arm of the settee as he leaned across to watch Joy spread her work on the middle cushion.

Instinctively Margaret shrank away from him, and checked herself instantly. It would not do to appear openly rude. Not that she cared what Dom might think, but she had no wish to offend Joy and Lex. The first instinctive liking she felt for them both had not diminished during the closer acquaintance of the evening, and she hoped they might become friends if they remained in the district long enough. And it was a thoughtful kindness on their part to invite Dom to balance the party. It was not their fault that she did not appreciate their choice of her supper partner.

'You haven't seen my latest effort yet, Sue.' Joy unrolled a large sheet of graph paper between them.

'It doesn't look much like embroidery to me.' Bill regarded it with male incomprehension.

'It isn't, yet,' Joy laughed. 'I'm working out a design for a tapestry.'

'Maggie specialises in tapestry,' Bill informed her, and Margaret scowled at his use of the hated nickname, but she could not hide her interest in what Joy had accomplished.

'I've done a little of my own designing, but not a lot,' she confessed. 'This is working up well. What are you taking your picture from?'

'Dom did a sketch for me. The harbour at Meldonmouth is so picturesque, I just had to have it on canvas. Wool and canvas, I mean,' Joy smiled. 'Dom heard me say so to Lex, and he presented me with this a week later. Isn't it lovely?'

It was a skilfully executed pen and ink drawing of the harbour. The long, curving wall was there, and the huddle of fishermen's cottages—Margaret could pick out her own quite clearly—with one or two boats drawn up on the shingle beach above the level of the tide. With the aid of Joy's skill, and her sensitive interpretation to bring the picture to life, it would work up into a particularly lovely tapestry.

'Why, that's your cottage—look, Margaret,' Sue pointed excitedly. 'The one with the shutters against the windows,' as Joy searched the sketch with an interested eye.

'Now you know where I live, you'll have to come round and see it at close quarters,' Margaret found herself saying. 'If you become familiar with the cottages and the harbour, you'll get the feel of it in your design, and you'll be able to see the change of colour and light at different hours of the day. You can choose the combination you like best for your picture, then. And of course, you can have a look at my tapestries at the same time,' she invited.

'They're worth looking at,' Bill assured his hostess solemnly. 'I know, I've inspected them myself.'

'Sue and Bill are often in and out,' Margaret pressed, 'we could have a return supper party. Or lunch and tea, if it's easier for you. You wouldn't have any problems with getting a baby-sitter then.' She stopped abruptly, aware too late of the trap she had set for herself, and stumbled into without a thought. She had invited her host and hostess and their tiny son to come along with Bill and his fiancé. Common courtesy demanded she should also invite Dom.

She swallowed convulsively, but the words she should have uttered—that good manners demanded she must utter, and quickly—stuck in her throat. She had met Dom three times, only once socially, and already he invaded her thoughts in a way she had begun to fear and resent. As irrationally, she resented her cottage being included in his sketch.

During the summer months, wandering artists frequently stopped to sketch or paint, and she did not mind. But the mere fact that Dom had sketched her home aroused her anger. From the exactitude and care with which his work was executed, it was obvious he must have spent a considerable time doing it. Meticulous attention to detail told her he had observed each outward facet of her house with keen perception—perhaps even while she herself had been at home, maybe visible to the watching, gentian-coloured eyes as she moved about the quiet rooms, appearing occasionally in front of the window, unconscious that her movements might be an open book to an interested observer. Even the thick walls of her cottage were no defence against this man, she thought resentfully.

'You'll have to fix it for when Lex and Dom are on leave from the rig,' Sue reminded her, and artlessly settled her difficulty at the same time. There was no way she could exclude Dom now.

'We're ashore for the next fornight,' Lex stated contentedly. 'Dom will probably trek backwards and forwards to the rig once or twice, worrying about his hydrocarbons,' he said tolerantly, 'but officially we're both on leave.' His expansive grin suggested he was well content with the arrangement. He dropped on to the arm of the settee behind Joy and rested his arm across her shoulders in a way that brought a quick smile to her face and a warmth to her liquid dark eyes. They were lucky, very lucky. Hastily Margaret turned her attention to what Bill was saying.

'Sunday's about the best day for us three,' the house surgeon suggested. 'We're pretty pushed during the week days, with Neil being away.'

'Let's make it next Sunday, then.' Margaret could not bring herself to invite Dom directly, to ask him in so many words to invade her home, tacitly giving her consent to his taking yet another step across the fine dividing line that separated Doctor Warrender the professional from Margaret Warrender the woman. Perhaps next Sunday he would make one of his unofficial visits to the rig, and so relieve her of his presence. Her hope was shortlived.

'I'll keep Sunday free,' the geologist promised gravely.

'If I get caught up in an emergency, Sue will deputise for me until I can get away. It's happened before,' Margaret warned, semi-apologising in advance in case she might not, after all, be at home when her guests arrived, and even as she spoke she found herself wondering bleakly how often in the recent past she had had to cancel arrangements at the last minute, disappointing others, until in the end she simply gave up making appointments for fear she might not be able to keep them, and so lost touch with her friends. Sue was quite right, Neil would have to come up with an extra pair of hands at the General, to relieve the workload. Though just for once, she thought ruefully, she would welcome being kept at the hospital. Anything to prevent her from having to spend the day in Dom's company. Perhaps someone would come in with an appendix, or.... No, it was wrong to wish trouble on someone else, merely to solve her own difficulties. She put the idea out of her mind with guilty haste.

'Have you chosen your wools yet?' she changed the subject, in case her omission to directly invite Dom should be noticed by the others.

'One or two, mainly the background colours.' Joy reached out and dipped her hand into a sewing box which Lex obligingly dragged close to her seat. 'Of course, it would be easier if the beach was a sandy one,' she grumbled good-humouredly. 'The pebbles seem to attract the light in so many different shades, it'll be difficult to get it right on the tapestry.'

'It's hard on Teddy having a pebbly beach, too,' Sue reminded his mother. 'I'm sure he'd prefer sand, where he could play with a bucket and spade.'

'I'll teach him to skim pebbles,' Bill suggested mischievously.

'You'll do nothing of the sort!' Lex sat upright indignantly. 'We won't have a window left in the house if you teach that young scamp to throw stones. He gets into enough trouble as it is, without even trying.'

'He's too little yet for us to worry about that,' Joy said comfortably. 'Though it would have been nice if he'd had the sand to play in. But I suppose that would have tempted him on to the beach, and the beach is near the water....' She counted her blessings philosophically. 'I thought these multi-shades of grey and white,' she held up a bundle of wool hanks for Margaret to inspect. 'They'll go with the white cottage walls.'

'You've got plenty of wool.' Margaret ran expert eyes over the bundle.

'I thought of doing a pair of pictures, not just one,' Joy explained. 'Both seascapes, or coastal scenes, something like that.'

'We're going to need a house twice this size if you keep on,' her husband protested. 'Have you seen the length this picture's going to be?' he demanded of them despairingly.

'Show me.' Margaret did not share his mock horror. She knew how Joy felt. It was good to tackle a formidable task, however long it might take to accomplish. It was something, so to speak, to make friends with—to plan for. A kind of anchor, no matter what the daily ups and downs, it would be there, waiting for the quiet hours. In Joy's nomad existence she must need such an anchor to give her some sense of continuity throughout her endless house moves, Margaret sensed perceptively.

'It's a long one, like Lex said.' Joy unrolled the canvas

and held out one end for Margaret to take. 'It's more in the nature of a picture panel.'

'What an unusual idea!' Margaret eyed the long, narrow strip of canvas enthusiastically. 'You've managed to get good canvas, too.' She rubbed the heel of her hand appreciatively across the squared material.

'Oh, bother!' She gave a click of annoyance. 'Hold it still for a moment, Joy,' she begged, 'the fastening of my watch bracelet seems to have caught on one of the end holes.' The semi-stiff stuff had pulled the catch open and left her watch dangling on her wrist.

'Has it done any damage?' Her hostess looked anxious.

'No, the fastening's worked loose,' Margaret reassured her. 'I've been meaning to get it fixed for some time, but things have been so busy at the General I haven't had the opportunity to take it to the jewellers. I must find time somehow, soon,' she murmured, 'I wouldn't lose it for anything. It was my parents' birthday gift.' She let the canvas roll back into Joy's fingers, and caught her watch just in time as it slipped from her wrist and fell on to her lap.

'It's a delicate fastening.' Dom leaned forward over the arm of the settee as she slipped the band back over her wrist, laying it flat on her lap to try and steady it while she manipulated the tiny links. Her fingers trembled at his sudden closeness, becoming clumsy with a fumbling ineffectiveness that never afflicted them in a professional emergency. She scorned herself that it should afflict them now, but although she bent all her will to keeping them steady, she seemed to have no power to force them to do as she wanted them to. Twice, three times, the slender strap slipped from her grasp, and she gave an exclamation of annoyance. She felt her cheeks grow hot, conscious of Dom watching her abortive efforts, which rising irritation made clumsier than before.

'For goodness' sake, look the other way, can't you?' she longed to shout at him, but instead she bit her lip and fumed in silence.

'Let me do it. You need two hands, with something so small as this.'

He leaned further across the settee arm, until his shoulder rested against her own. She started violently as his fingers touched her wrist, and felt him pause in his self-appointed task, and turn and look at her, but she kept her eyes fixed resolutely downwards, determined not to meet his look, burningly conscious of the betraying warmth that rose in a pink tide up the slender column of her throat and stained her cheeks, and which she knew from the quick turn of his head had not gone unnoticed by her helper.

She tried to appear cool and indifferent, but in spite of herself her hand made an involuntary movement away from his touch, just as he snapped the catch closed.

'Oh! It's pinching me.' The pain was sharp as the catch caught the soft flesh of her wrist, and he instantly snapped it open again.

'You should have kept your hand still, it wouldn't have pinched you then.' She got no more sympathy from him than the roustabout had done, and indignation bubbled inside her, even though honesty told her what he said was perfectly true. It was her own fault, but she was in no mood to forgive him on that account. The stain of embarrassment in her cheeks turned to a deeper hue, of anger.

'It's. . . .'

The shrill summons of a telephone bell interrupted her.

'Who can that be, at this time on a Sunday evening?' Joy wondered, and Bill gave an anticipatory groan.

'What's the betting it's the hospital?' he asked dolefully. 'Keep your fingers crossed for us,' as Lex reached for the receiver.

'Yes, he's here. Sorry, Bill,' Lex echoed his guest's disappointment. 'It's for you,' he confirmed.

'Mmm . . . yes . . . don't worry, Sister, I'll be along right away.' The house surgeon shrugged resignedly and put the receiver back on its hook. 'Sorry, folks, but I'll have to leave you.'

'I'll come along, and wait for you.' Sue was already on her feet, gathering up her handbag. 'That way at least we can spend the rest of the evening together, if it's only in your office,' she said ruefully.

'What is it, Bill?' Margaret forgot her wrist, even forgot Dom and his shoulder still touching her own, her whole attention was concentrated on her colleague.

'Relax,' he told her easily, 'it's only a broken wrist, no complications. There's no need for you to spoil your evening as well. I can cope, you've had to take all the pressure up to now, since Neil's been away. It's my turn tonight.'

'But....' She had come in Bill's car, and would much prefer to go back with him. At least the house surgeon did not have the same disconcerting effect on her that the geologist aroused.

'I'll run you home,' Dom reacted as she feared he might. 'You cut along if you must,' he told Bill, 'I'll see Margaret safely back for you.'

'Thanks,' Bill accepted gratefully, and Margaret could have hit him. Between the two of them, she thought furiously, they were treating her like a parcel that had to be delivered, and had no say in the means by which that delivery was to be accomplished. But if they had both been at the hospital, Bill would have taken the op as normal routine, and if she insisted on coming along as well it would make it look, at least to the others, as if she did not trust him.

'You do understand, don't you?' Sue begged their indulgence for deserting the supper party with her fiancé.

'Of course we do,' Joy assured her goodnaturedly. 'Remember, we know what it's like to try and snatch an hour or two together. I only see Lex for two weeks out of every four. Entertain Margaret for us for a minute or two, Dom, while we go and see Bill and Sue off,' she continued, as she followed Sue out of the room in search of coats.

'I'll come and back you out in the car, the street's narrow just here,' Lex offered, and to Margaret's dismay he, too, went with Bill, and left herself and Dom alone in the room.

'How would you like me to entertain you?'

Sardonic amusement lit the blue eyes, and panic rose in Margaret's throat as he quit his chair and, deftly removing Joy's embroidery materials to the top of her workbox, lowered himself on to the settee beside her.

'T-tell me about your work,' she stammered the first thing that came into her head, and the sardonic gleam deepened.

'Like Joy said, I'm a geologist,' he drawled. 'My activities are channelled more or less into the role of a sort of oil detective.' He paused politely, and she searched wildly for something to say to answer him. Why couldn't he just keep on talking? she wondered desperately. Most people, given such an invitation, would have needed no urging. She felt angrily certain that Dom, by his silence, was deliberately goading her.

'Joy says it's dangerous,' she babbled at last, when he still declined to speak.

'There's more danger from the politicking in the Boardroom than there is on the rig itself,' he said drily, and Margaret remembered Lex's comment.

'Your career could be at stake over this. . . .'

So despite his outward confidence he was not unaware of the hazards, she thought shrewdly, and felt convinced that in spite of the high stake he would manoeuvre like a poker player, checkmating with consummate skill each move the opposition made against him, pitting knowledge, and that extra sixth sense which Lex said he possessed, against the weight of united opposition, enjoying the thrill of the challenge, until he triumphed, as she knew he would. As he must! her heart suddenly cried out, taking her by surprise by its vehemence.

'There's really no need for you to take me home,' she burst into urgent speech as the silence began to lengthen again. 'I always walk back when I'm on late night duty. It isn't far.' Speech was a sort of defence, to keep him—or her own thoughts, she did not know which—at bay. And she needed the walk tonight, on her own, to quieten the mad turmoil that was going on between her head and her heart.

'It's impossible,' said her head.

'It's happened,' responded her heart.

And trembling, she listened to the two, and did not know which one to believe. Dom spoke again.

'It may not be far from the hospital, but the cottages at the end of the harbour are too far to walk from here, particularly in heels like those.'

He cast a critical glance at the peep-toes and tapering four-inch heels of her patent leather slippers, daintily suitable for the new, longer length of her dress, but disastrous for traversing the steeply sloping cobbled streets of the town that led down to the harbour, and her home. She had forgotten the sketch, and the fact that, because of it, he now knew where she lived, even which cottage of the number huddled at the end of the harbour.

'You certainly can't walk home tonight.' Joy came back and overheard her remark. 'The wind's rising quite strongly, it looks as if there's another storm blowing up.'

'They seem to be a speciality in this area,' Lex commented, following his wife indoors.

'We get one about every four or five days at this time of the year,' Margaret agreed absently. She felt she would even welcome battling against a storm, high heels or no high heels, it would suit her mood tonight. Nothing the weather could produce could possibly equal the storm that was going on inside her, in which her head and her heart seemed to be taking opposing sides. And trapped between the two, she could only wonder helplessly which one was likely to win.

CHAPTER FIVE

His car was a surprise.

If she had thought about it at all, she would have supposed a geologist would drive a rather sober vehicle—something practical, perhaps vaguely battered. But then she had always imagined geologists to be old. A slight smile touched her lips in the windy darkness. Even geologists must be young some time. This one was about her own age. Two years older, she discovered later; he was thirty last birthday. And his car was the reverse of sober.

It was a long, low, and extremely powerful-looking two-seater sports car. Fervently she wished this particular geologist conformed to her preconceived notions. The close intimacy of an enclosed two-seater was the last kind of transport she wanted to share with Dom, but it appeared she had no alternative.

He drew up at the base of the short flight of steps that led to their host's house, and instead of waiting for her to join him he removed his long length from behind the wheel and ran back up the steps to join her and escort her back to the car with an old-fashioned courtesy that took her by surprise. Her meetings with Dominic Orr up to now had not led her to expect gallantry from him.

'It's been a lovely evening. . . .'

'Mind how you go!'

'We're looking forward to next Sunday. . . .'

With a final wave they were on their way. The long hood nosed through the narrow, steep streets, taking the hair-raising bends with infinite care. Her escort seemed to be in no particular hurry to discharge his duties and be gone. She wished he might be. Once more, the silence lengthened between them until it became intolerable. In

51

any other sports car, she thought, irritable with tension, the noise of the engine would have made speech impossible. This one was as much of a surprise as its owner. The voice from beneath the hood was no more than a well-bred purr, and her companion seemed quite content to remain silent for the rest of the drive.

'Have you known Lex for long?'

It sounded trite, perhaps even a little impertinent, since he was a close friend of the Nobles, and she was, as yet, merely an acquaintance. But she had to say something to break the silence, or burst.

'Just over ten years.' His face was a sharply etched silhouette in the darkness, the planes of his jaw uncompromisingly square against the paler darkness of the windscreen. 'We were at university together,' he volunteered without turning his head, his eyes intent on the road unwinding in front of them.

'And you both chose oil exploration for a career. Isn't that rather unusual?'

'Why?' he enquired, but not as if he really cared what her answer might be. The fact that he had chosen oil as his career would be sufficient for him, she thought bitingly. She doubted if the oil companies themselves had any say in the matter!

'Engineering and geology make natural partners for oil,' he continued, as if it should have been self-evident, and she felt affronted by his tone, her intelligence questioned. He spoke in the manner he might have used to explain something to Teddy, she thought indignantly. 'They're as old as the earth, and as new as tomorrow, the same as the treasure we seek,' he added unexpectedly.

She glanced up at him sharply. His voice changed, it became soft, reflective, as if he might have spoken the last sentence to himself rather than to her. As if he was merely voicing his thoughts aloud. The sensitive, almost poetic description of his own and Lex's work was oddly at variance with the Dominic Orr Margaret had come to expect—as unexpected as his almost olde-worlde courtesy earlier, as unexpected as his car. Against her will, she felt intrigued. He was a strange mixture, this flaxen-haired giant with the gentian-coloured eyes. Strange, and wholly disconcerting.

'Your cottage is the one with the shutters, isn't it?'

They had arrived. Already. She sat up in her seat, startled, and was confronted by the familiar huddle of cottages as Dom swung the car parallel with them and braked to a halt. The journey that she had feared nervously would go on for ever was over, and she had not even noticed.

'Your cottage is the one with the shutters, isn't it?'

He repeated his question, and turned right round in the driving seat to look at her, awaiting her answer. Perversely, she wished more than one of the cottages possessed shutters, if only to confuse him, to topple some of the air of self-assured rightness that rode him, and had the power to exasperate her more than anything—or anyone she had ever before encountered.

'Yes, it's the one with the shutters.'

It was useless to deny it, since Sue had pointed it out to Joy on the sketch, and the dark oblongs of stoutly slatted wood stood out like banners on the whitewashed walls.

'I'll have to close them before I go inside. Goodness, I'd no idea the wind was so strong!' she exclaimed. 'Joy said there was a storm blowing up.' She gasped as the force of the wind hit her like a physical blow when Dom strode round the long hood of the car and opened the passenger door to help her out. The wind was just as rough when they left their host and hostess, but although their house was higher than her own, it had the advantage of being sheltered by the other buildings in the town. Here, next to the shore, with nothing but the sea wall between them and the wild waters of the Firth, the wind seemed set to blow her over. Helped by the uneven cobbles and her unaccustomed high heels, it nearly succeeded, and she staggered against Dom as she rose from the shelter of the car.

'Hold on to me.'

He slammed the car door shut and pulled her against him, keeping his arm round her to shelter her with his own body from the force of the next gust. She froze into stillness under his grasp. His arm felt hard against her, even through the generous folds of her cape, and his hold set up an instant tingling through her veins, an awareness of the masterful strength of him that defied, nay even enjoyed the wildness of the elements.

She stiffened away from him, started to pull herself free, and then the gust died and his arm dropped from round her, no longer needed as a support. And it could have been the one, or it could have been the other, which caught her breath in what might have been the suggestion of a sob. Regardless of her heels, she turned away from him and ran blindly towards the house.

'I'll close the shutters before I go in. Don't let me detain you,' she called over her shoulder, but instead of him getting into the car and driving away as she hoped he would—as she hoped he wouldn't—she did not know what she hoped, she thought desperately—his footsteps crunched on the cobbles behind her, and she struggled with the shutter fastening as if it was stuck to her hand. He must not put his arm round her again, not even to steady her against the wind. His touch sent a strange, wild singing through her veins, like nothing she had ever experienced before. It matched the wild, free note of the wind, until she felt she was being borne along with it like an autumn leaf before a gale, with neither the ability nor the will to control where it might take her.

Hastily she worked the bolt that held the shutter to the wall, keeping her back to him, not looking round. She clung to the bolt as if it was a lifebelt in a sea as stormy as that which thundered and crashed against the harbour wall. A sea that, despite its terrors, had waters as blue as gentians, into the depths of which she dared not let herself gaze, for fear they might engulf her. . . .

'I'll do it for you.' In two swift strides he was beside her. Why didn't he get back into his car, and go away? 'You won't hold the shutters in this wind.'

'I can manage.' She gave the bolt an urgent wrench.

'It's jammed.' He raised his hand to take it from her.

'No, it's coming.' She held on to it stubbornly. 'Oh!' It freed itself without any warning, sliding back suddenly along its sharp metal track and bringing her hand back with it. She felt the hard, unyielding point of the track end cut deep into the base of her thumb; felt a warm wetness that smarted unbearably, and drew her breath in a sharp hiss of mingled pain and exasperation.

The pain made her release her grip on the bolt, and instantly the wind tore the shutter from her grasp. It caught the slatted wood like a sail and slammed it hard against the wall, then bounced it back again almost into Margaret's face. She felt the draught of it as it passed her head, then Dom's hands grabbed her and dragged her back out of the way of its returning path. He pulled her backwards without ceremony, ducking out of the way of the heavy, wildly swinging wood, that had it caught either of them would undoubtedly have caused serious injury. As it was, she merely lost one of her shoes as he clasped her bodily to him, half lifting, half dragging her across the cobbles.

'Did it hit you?' His voice was taut.

'No, it missed,' she managed to gasp. Thanks to Dom, but she did not say that. She hadn't the breath. Even a blow from the shutter could not have such a devastating effect on her senses, she thought bemusedly. They reeled from the feel of the lean, muscular hardness of him against her, his arms right round her in a vicelike grip that pressed her face into the fine wool of his perfectly tailored jacket. Faintly she could smell something astringent, like talc, or it could have been a discreet after-shave lotion.

'Let me go!' she panted. Her heart hammered, and she tried to tell herself it was because of her narrow escape, but even to herself it did not sound convincing. She tried to struggle upright, ineffectually, she was no match for the strength of his hold. 'I can stand. I'm not hurt.' Desperation lent her voice a sharpness that must have penetrated, because he eased his arms from around her and stood her on her feet.

'Did the bolt cut you?' Could he see the handkerchief she pressed to her thumb, habit making her react to cover the wound?

'It's only a scratch.' Her voice lost some of its wobble as he set her on her feet, though he still supported her with one hand against the force of the erratic gusts.

'Put your shoe on.' He reached down, groped, found it and set it down beside her foot, then bent to guide her toes into the slender length of it. She curled them in protest at his touch and saw his teeth gleam momentarily in the darkness, his fair head tilted as he turned his face up towards her, then the shutter slammed back against the wall with a clatter that jerked him upright.

'Go and stand in the shelter of the doorway, while I close the shutters for you.' He gave her a slight push towards the porch. 'I'll go and get my flashlight from the car.'

'Go and stand there yourself,' she gritted ferociously beneath her breath, her independent spirit rising in revolt at his authoritative tone. As second in command to Neil Venables at the General, she was more accustomed to giving instructions than to receiving them.

Another shrieking gust rattled the shutters at their moorings and ballooned her cape round her in a manner that, for one terrifying second, made her wonder if it might lift her bodily from the ground.

'Dom!' His name rose to her lips in a panic-stricken plea, but the wind carried the sound away, and she turned lest she be tempted to call out to him again, groping her way along the wall with her uninjured hand until she gained the comparative shelter of the minute porch with a gasp of relief.

From behind her she heard the bolts of the shutters clang to, then the car door slam shut. Dom must have found the flashlight. He was coming back! With fingers that shook she snapped open the clasp of her handbag. If she could find her key quickly enough, she could have the door open, and herself inside the house, by the time he gained the porch, and could confront him with a cool goodnight from the sanctuary of her own hallway. In spite of the storm, she was determined not to ask him inside. The party on the following Sunday would be quite soon enough for that, she decided grimly. The way she felt now, it would take her the rest of the week to regain her composure.

She held her bag with her one hand and fumbled for her key with the other, and felt the handkerchief slip away from her cut thumb. She gave an exclamation of annoyance and tried to ignore it, but she could not ignore the warm wetness that crept across her hand again the moment the pressure was removed from the impromptu pad, nor the imminent danger it presented to the so far unsoiled whiteness of her cape if she allowed it to spread. In her haste to replace the handkerchief over the cut, she nearly dropped her handbag.

'Give me your bag, I'll find your key for you.' There was a click and a swathe of white light cut across the darkness from the powerful flashlight Dom held. He directed it straight on to her hand, revealing the stained handkerchief. Margaret balled her fingers into a fist, trying to hide it from him, but she was too late, he had already noticed all there was to see.

'I can manage.'

'If you want to risk getting bloodstains all over your cape...?' His voice was curt, on the edge of impatience.

'No—no, I don't.' The cape was new and expensive, and this was the first time she had had an opportunity to wear it. She capitulated unwillingly. Once he found the key and let her into the house he would go, she thought with relief. Reluctantly she held out her handbag to him. She felt him glance at her as he took it, but she refused to meet his look.

'The key's somewhere in the bottom.' It would have taken her no time at all to find it, she knew the feel of it, but he would have to search. She did not relish the thought of him searching the intimate, personal possessions in her bag.

'What a clutter!' He turned his flashlight on to the contents, and unexpectedly a laugh shook him. His lips tilted upwards in an amused arc in the flashlight. 'You're just like any other woman,' he exclaimed. As if he had made some new discovery, like his oil, Margaret thought furiously. She half expected him to shout Eureka!

'Did you expect me to have two heads or something?' she asked him icily. She resented the implication that she was incapable of being anything other than an automaton inside a white starched coat. Almost as much as she resented the small, barely audible whisper inside her that said she did not want to be just like any other woman to Dom. She wanted to be something special.... She reined in her thoughts hastily. She must be mad! It was the storm ... or the unexpected evening out, or. ...

'No, I expected a doctor to be a bit tidier, that's all,' he grinned, and added with disconcerting perception, 'but I forgot, you're not a doctor tonight, are you? You're just Margaret—for tonight?' He stopped rummaging for a minute, and his eyes met hers in the reflected half light from the flashlight beam, locked them in a penetrating look that melted the remnants of her armour; denied its existence, in fact, laughing at its puny inability to offer her any protection against the forceful, dominant maleness of him, pressed against her in the confines of the tiny porchway, his head bent close down above her own. Would he...? She caught her breath. No! He must not. She raised her hands instinctively to her face, warding off she refused to think what, and the move brought his eyes back to her hand, and the stained handkerchief covering it.

'The quicker you get that properly dressed, the better.' He returned to his task with renewed zest, and a complete disregard for the contents of her handbag, she thought indignantly. 'The bolt track was probably rusty as well,' he offered uncaring criticism at her probable lack of maintenance of her property. 'Got it!'

He fished out the key with the St Christopher key ring attached, and dangled it in front of her triumphantly. She saw him glance at the key ring before he inserted the key in the lock. His eyes seemed to miss nothing. By now he had probably registered the fact that she used a clear lip-salve, and favoured Blue Grass perfume, she thought sourly, and felt a quick sense of relief when he opened the door, extracted the key, and dropped it back among the clutter, as he called it, in her bag. He snapped the catch shut and handed it back to her with a derisive bow.

'Thank you for bringing me home.'

She accepted it stiffly. She stepped ahead of him into the hall, and immediately turned, and if he had done what she intended he would have remained on the porch, made a polite rejoinder, and taken his leave. Typically, he did not conform to her plan. He walked right in after her, and she had to step back hastily to give him room.

'I didn't. . . .' she began indignantly, and he stood over her looking down at her in the brighter lamplight of the hanging light on the hall ceiling.

'Didn't invite me in? I know,' he said imperturbably. 'But I'm coming, just the same. I want to see how bad that cut is on your hand. If I left you, and you bled to death in the night, I should get the blame.' His voice, his eyes, held a mocking lilt, as if he cared more whether he would get the blame, than if she bled to death. As if he did not really care about either. She flushed angrily.

'As a doctor, I'm more than capable of taking care of my own cuts,' she informed him frigidly.

'Not necessarily,' he returned easily, in no way put out by her snub. 'Remember the cobbler's children,' he reminded her, and followed close on her heels as she turned towards the kitchen. As he moved, he reached out a long arm and slammed the front door behind them. The old-fashioned thickness of it effectively shut out the noise of the storm, helped by the closed shutters across the front windows, and suddenly the silence in the cottage seemed oppressive. Margaret had not noticed it before. She could hear her own breathing, and Dom's soft footsteps on the carpet just behind her.

'Do you have shutters to the back windows as well?' He spoke close into her ear.

'No. The back of the house is sheltered. It's only the front, facing the harbour, that catches the full force of the wind.'

They were talking as if they were making polite conversation at a vicarage tea-party, she thought half hysterically, and sat down abruptly on a handy stool.

'Don't tell me a doctor feels faint at the sight of blood?' His voice jeered at her. It seemed to come from a long way off, but the derision in it acted like a shower of cold water. Perhaps it was intended to . . . .

'Don't be ridiculous,' she snapped, sharper than was actually necessary, because his words struck uncomfortably close to the truth, though it was not the cut that was making her knees feel peculiar. It just served as a handy excuse. 'I just want to get out of these high heels, that's all.'

She kicked her shoes off, to give an added ring of truth to her words, and immediately wished she had kept them on. The heels gave her added height, which boosted her fast disappearing self-confidence. Without them, the tip of her red-gold curls barely came up to the breast pocket of Dom's jacket. It was a tactical error on her part, and an amused glint in his eyes told her he was aware of the fact.

'Keep your hanky over your thumb, I'll undo your cape for you.' He took over. May as well try to stem the tide, Margaret thought helplessly. There was nothing left for her to do, except remain still while his fingers manipulated the fastening at her throat with surprising dexterity. He had long, slender hands, the hands of a musician, and she wondered vaguely if he played an instrument. She tried to think which instrument would best suit him. To think about anything was better than letting her thoughts dwell on the fact that his hand was brushing against her chin as he undid the fastening of her cape.

'Stand up.'

He drew the cloak away from her shoulders as she slipped obediently off the stool, and draped the folds carefully across his arm, not clumsily bunching it, as most men would have done.

'Now ease your hand through the arm slot.' He held the material apart to prevent it from brushing against her hand, then draped the garment over the back of a chair, out of the way.

'Let me see your thumb.'

He took hold of her hand without waiting for her to say yes or no. The cut had stopped bleeding, but the handkerchief had stuck to it, and she winced as he pulled it away.

'Now you've started it up again!'

Sudden tears welled in her eyes at the sharpness of it, and she turned swiftly, groping towards the sink, her one thought to hide them from him. With a quick flick she set the tap running and thrust her hands, both of them, underneath the stream. The shock of the cold water steadied her. It cleared her thoughts and brought back a measure of her customary self-control. Dom might be in charge of whatever he did on the oil rig, she thought mutinously, but she, Margaret, was in charge of herself in her own home, and high heels or no high heels, it was time he realised that.

'You ought to have an anti-tet jab for that,' he began.

'I'm covered in that respect,' she informed him crisply,

her confidence returning with a rush, and to her relief her
voice once more held the sure control of Doctor Warrender.
Gone, for the moment anyway, was the wavering uncertainty of Margaret.

'The evening's over,' she told herself firmly. It was time
for Margaret, like Cinderella, to creep back to the obscurity
where she belonged, and for Dominic Orr to understand
that she was not, in fact, just like any other woman, to be
bowled over by superlative good looks, and willing to give
in to his dictatorial manner because of them.

The evening was definitely over.

It helped, she found, if she kept repeating it to herself.
There was next Sunday still to come, but that was a whole
week away. She could put it out of her mind for the moment, anyway. She smoothed a plaster dressing matter-of-
factly over the cut.

'Ah, yes, I'd forgotten you would be—Doctor Warrender.'

His own tone changed, matching hers, catching her
change of mood as easily as a barometer catches a change in
temperature. He was extraordinarily perceptive—far too
perceptive for her comfort.

'Oh, well,' he shrugged, 'it was a pleasant evening while
it lasted.'

So he, too, accepted that it was over. Contrarily, a flat
feeling possessed her, a drab sense of anti-climax, like going
back to work following Christmas, or the day after a wed-
ding. She was Doctor Warrender again, no longer Margaret.
She flashed him a quick glance. It was humiliating to have
to tilt her head so far back to look at him, but without her
shoes on she had no option. She saw to her chagrin that
there was a glint of laughter lurking in his eyes.

'Very pleasant,' she agreed stiffly. 'But it's time to say
goodnight.'

She meant to be crushing, to send him on his way feeling
as deflated, if possible, as she felt herself. But Dominic
Orr was not the type to respond in the conventionally ac-

cepted manner. She should have known that.

'So it is.' A slow grin lifted his lips, and sudden panic caught her by the throat. 'I'd forgotten.' He flicked a glance at his wrist watch. 'It isn't midnight yet, though, Cinderella,' he murmured, and reached out towards her.

She tried to step back, but the kitchen was tiny and Dom's arms were long, and she came up against the hard, unyielding edge of the cupboard worktop.

'Goodnight, Margaret. Thank you for a lovely evening.'

His words mocked her. Words he knew she would have used on him, stiffly formal, designed to keep him at a distance. A safe distance. His lips were the reverse of formal, and they did not remain at a distance. He gathered her to him, lifted her free of the floor as easily as if she had been a child, so that she had no leverage to back away from him, and his flaxen head bent unhurriedly over her. She raised her face in protest, and his lips brushed her mouth. This time she could not raise her hands to cover her face, her arms were pinioned under his hands, so she did the only thing that was left to her, and twisted her face to one side, out of his reach.

Instead of releasing her, his lips continued to explore, seeking the sweetly perfumed spot behind her ear, pressing one red-gold curl against it before passing on down the slender column of her throat. Starting again the wild singing in her veins that she would fain not hear again. That she dared not allow herself to listen to.... She had to stop him, somehow. With her arms pinioned, there was only one way open to her, and she took it.

She kicked him. Hard. With all her strength, she drove her feet against his shins. She forgot she had no shoes on, and the softness of her toes met hard, muscular legs; as hard and lean as the rest of him, and she gasped as they punished her feet for their temerity.

'For two pins, I'd spank you for that.'

He held her away from him, still above the floor, so that she could not run away, as her panting breath and wildly dilated eyes told him she longed to do.

'You wouldn't dare!' Her eyes flashed green fire, and she started to struggle, desperate to free herself from his hold. 'Go away and tame your wildcat well!' she shouted at him furiously. 'You can't tame me that way.'

Although she knew it would hurt her more than it hurt him, and although caution warned her that he was quite capable of carrying out his threat to spank her, she kicked him again, and felt her earlier panic turn to cold fear as his face changed, whitened, and went grim.

'There are more ways than one of taming a wildcat,' he gritted through clenched teeth.

He dropped her none too gently back on to her feet on the floor, but he did not let her go. She twisted and tried to break away, but he held her without apparent effort, pulling her close against him. One lean hand came under her chin, tilting her face up to his, holding her so that she could not escape. And this time his lips did not brush lightly against her own. They clamped down with an unmerciful pressure, fired by the anger that rode him, darkening his eyes until they turned almost black. Margaret shivered uncontrollably. This was worse than she had feared. She could not breathe. She could not break free. And worst of all, she discovered she did not want to.

Against her will she found herself responding, returning the hard pressure of his lips with tremulous seeking, her body becoming pliant in his arms, so that he no longer had to use force to hold her. At last he raised his head.

'Dom. . . .' The whisper came through her softly parted lips, pleading, beseeching. . . .

'Goodnight, Margaret. Thank you for a lovely evening.' His voice mocked, but deep in the gentian blue eyes flared a strange, unreadable expression, and she dropped her own, unable to meet them.

'Stay for a coffee,' she heard herself falter.

'If I stay, I may want more from you than a coffee,' he grated harshly, and pushed her from him roughly.

Her head snapped up, angry, shaken. Fearful? But all she caught sight of was the broad, dark shape of his back, disappearing through the front door.

The howl of the storm outside roared through the opening, like a wild beast in search of prey, then Dom pulled the door shut behind him, muting its anger. Margaret heard his car door slam, the engine start, and twin beams from his headlights raked across the windows. Then they were gone, leaving her alone in the darkened hall, battling with a storm of emotion that was wilder than anything the elements could produce.

It was a storm, she realised despairingly, from which she could find no shelter, other than the shelter of Dom's arms.

CHAPTER SIX

'THANK goodness it's Monday!'

Margaret stifled a yawn, and pulled a hurried brush through her hair. She did not need the clock to tell her she had slept late. A dismayed awareness of daylight filtering through the curtains stampeded her out of bed and through her dressing in record time. She wriggled into her skirt and pulled her sweater over her head with scant regard for the way they looked. She could tidy up if she got a break during the morning. In the meantime, her white coat would cover any deficiencies.

Her white coat....

For a moment her eyes lingered on the soft green folds of her dress of the evening before, tossed across the back of a chair, with the high-heeled slippers forlorn on the carpet underneath. Margaret's slippers.... Well, she was not Margaret this morning, she was Doctor Warrender, she reminded herself firmly, so——

'Thank goodness it's Monday!'

'I need a daily dose of ward rounds and casualty work to put me to rights,' she prescribed for herself out loud, without bothering to diagnose what it was that ailed her. She refused to probe into that particular malaise. Dom was the cause, and the effect had been to keep her awake until the small hours of the morning, with the result that if she did not hurry she would be late starting her rounds at the General.

'How did your concussion case go last night? The one you left the party for?' she countered Bill's cheery 'Good morning' and obvious desire to stop for a chat, and reached for the clean white coat that was hung ready in her office when she got there. Five minutes early. She glanced at the bland face of the clock above the casualty department entrance and felt a wave of gratitude for the kindly neighbour who gave her a lift in his van, and on learning she was late, promptly went out of his way to drive her right to the hospital entrance.

'It's saved you a rough walk,' her Good Samaritan excused his kindly action. 'The storm doesn't show much sign of abating, does it?'

The wind was, if anything, even stronger than the previous evening. It had risen to a crescendo during the night, had spent itself of its worst fury by the time daylight came, but with a knowledge born of experience Margaret feared it was only a temporary respite. Already the gusts were beginning to build up again in increasing frequency and violence, and it was this, combined with her late rising, that made her leave the shutters closed when she quitted the house. The continuing fury of the storm would make it bad on the oil rig. But perhaps Dom had remained ashore, after all? He was supposed to be on leave. Resolutely she closed her mind to the possibility that he might have done as Lex suggested, and gone out to the rig, even now be there in the teeth of the gale. Perhaps in danger ...

'It wasn't concussion,' Bill spoke patiently, 'it was a

broken wrist. I told you at the time.' He had told her, and she had forgotten. The party seemed like a million years ago now.

'By the way,' the house surgeon added, 'Neil rang just before you got here.'

'Drat the man!' Margaret's jangled nerves exploded in an exclamation of vexation. 'Why couldn't he wait until I got here?'

'You're always here early.' Bill's eyebrows lifted in surprise at her unexpected reaction. 'He had no reason to suppose this morning would be any different,' he pointed out reasonably.

'I know,' she felt contrite. 'I'm tired, I suppose,' she excused herself, 'after last night ...' She stopped abruptly. She could not explain to Bill about last night.

'It's the shock of having a few hours off for a change, I expect,' Bill said drily. To her relief, he seemed to accept that it was the party that might have tired her, not what happened afterwards. He could not know about what happened afterwards. 'That will soon alter,' he went on cheerily, 'Neil reckons he'll be back here by Sunday, and with another doctor in tow as well,' he said triumphantly. 'That means you and I can turn into human beings again, instead of machines. And you can plan your party for next Sunday after all, Maggie,' he smiled.

'That's all I need!' she exclaimed wrathfully, unable to help herself. 'There's no earthly reason why I can't work on Sunday as usual. Neil will need a rest after his journey, and the new doctor will want to settle in.' Too late, it dawned on her just how peculiar her attitude must seem to her companion. Unwelcoming, even, since he and Sue were invited to her party as well. She became conscious that the house surgeon was eyeing her strangely.

'Did Dom see you home last night?' he asked, a mite too casually.

'Yes.' It came out clipped, unencouraging, and totally uninformative. She ignored Bill's puzzled look and glanced ostentatiously at her watch, but he did not immediately move towards the door.

'You're five minutes early for your rounds,' he pointed out, and added with a hint of warning in his tone, 'You've got time to calm down before you go on the wards.'

'Calm down? I am calm.' Margaret did not realise she was quite so transparent. If she was not careful, Bill might begin to suspect why. His eyes were shrewd, and he had worked with her for long enough to know when something disturbed her. It was high time she took herself in hand.

In the event, her work did that for her. Without any effort on her part it exerted its usual discipline, and from her first word with the first ward Sister she encountered on her morning rounds the supper party, Dom, and all that happened afterwards dropped from her like a discarded cloak. Once more she was securely back inside her armour.

The telephone bell jolted her out of it again just as she started to eat a hasty sandwich that had to serve as elevenses and lunch.

'What a morning!' She sank on to the edge of her desk with a cup of coffee in one hand and a cheese roll in the other. 'Delayed in the wards, and then the storm had to blow those slates off the greengrocer's roof straight on to the people waiting for the bus.'

'It was lucky there weren't any worse injuries,' Sister Casualty took advantage of Margaret's inviting nod, and joined her.

'You'd think they'd have the sense to nail the slates down in an area like this,' Margaret grumbled. 'We get enough storms at this time of the year for the local builders to know what it's like.'

'They do, normally,' Sister sipped her own drink appreciatively. 'But the wind got suddenly worse, so the foreman brought the men off the roof for safety's sake, and the young apprentice they'd got with them didn't think to mention he'd left a dozen or so slates unnailed, still up there.'

'I suppose we ought to be thankful it wasn't a whole roof full,' Margaret rejoined ruefully. 'By the way, where's Doctor Quinn?' She missed Bill for the first time. 'I suppose he's already had his elevenses?'

'He only had time for a quick bite,' Sister grinned, 'then an appendix case came in, and he's in the operating theatre now.'

'Poor Bill,' Margaret sympathised, 'and it looks as if Sue will have to eat another solitary lunch. I'll try and join her, if I'm free.'

'It doesn't sound as if you're going to have time to finish your cheese roll, let alone eat lunch,' Sister Casualty said drily as a series of frantic bleeps sounded from the top pocket of Margaret's white overall.

'Just my luck,' she groaned. 'Oh, do shut up!' She flicked an irritable finger at the contraption, and the noise ceased. 'I wonder what's gone wrong now?' She picked up the telephone receiver. 'Doctor Warrender here. Wh-a-a-t?' She listened aghast to the brisk voice at the other end of the line. 'Yes—yes, tell them we'll get someone out to them, somehow.' She put the receiver back on the rest and turned despairingly to Sister Casualty.

'This is the limit!' she exclaimed. 'The oil rig has just radio-telephoned to say that they want a doctor flown out there right away. As if we can produce doctors out of a hat ...! I was afraid this might happen, when Mr Venables agreed to provide back-up services.'

'Wait for Doctor Quinn to come out of theatre, and send him,' Sister suggested.

'I daren't delay. If Bill hits trouble while he's operating, he might be ages, and the rig call could be urgent.' Margaret spoke as much to herself as to her companion, voicing her dilemma aloud.

'I thought they had their own doctor on the rig?'

'So they have. Apparently he's one of the casualties. Something to do with the storm last night, the operator said.' Margaret drummed worried fingers on the desk top, thinking swiftly. 'I'll have to go out there myself,' she decided reluctantly.

'But who's to cover Casualty, if you go?' Sister cried her concern. 'We've only got the young houseman left.'

'I'll ring Doctor Rollason.' Margaret picked up the receiver again, her mind made up. 'What a profession!' she gloomed. 'Ralph Rollason's only been retired for six months, and even in that short time he's already been called back here three times as a stand-in. And we sent him off with a new set of golf clubs to use.' The irony of their gift struck her, not for the first time. 'The poor man's scarcely had a chance to try them out yet.' She frowned anxiously. 'I hope to goodness he's not on the links now ... oh, Ralph,' as the ringing tone ceased, and a deep male voice sounded in her ear, 'thank goodness you're home! Yes, we do want you, and quickly,' she confirmed his rueful prediction. 'I've got to go out right away on an emergency call.' For a brief, desperate second she felt tempted to ask Ralph Rollason to go in her stead. The last thing she wanted was to go out to the oil rig, perhaps come face to face with Dom again. But Ralph was past retiring age. It would not be fair.

'No, I can't,' she muttered, then, 'sorry, I was thinking out loud,' she apologised. 'Bill can't go, either,' she explained to the unlucky retiree, 'he's in theatre, and with this storm blowing, anything might happen. We've already had most of a bus line-up in here this morning with their heads dented by slates from the greengrocer's roof.' She paused as gruff tones sounded from the other end of the line. 'Bless you, Ralph!' she exclaimed, and put the receiver down.

'Doctor Rollason will be here in under ten minutes,' she told Sister briskly. 'I'll go and grab my bag and a car, and get out to the air-strip. Whoever radioed in said a helicopter would be waiting.'

'You can't go up in one of those things, in this weather!' Sister Casualty sounded scandalised.

'Well, I certainly can't swim out to the rig,' Margaret hoped she sounded happier than she felt. 'It looks as if I might have to, though,' she thought to herself with some disquiet about half an hour later as she sat beside the pilot in the big Chinook and watched the grey cliffs give way to green heaving water underneath, flecked by foam blowing off the high wave tops in white streaks, along the direction of the wind. She cast a glance at the pilot. He was young, tough-looking, with a distinct American accent, and he owned a head of reassuringly brown hair.

She was nearly at the airport before it occurred to her that Dom might be piloting the helicopter that was waiting to take her out to the rig. It was no use arguing to herself that Dom was a geologist, not a pilot. He did use the helicopter, when it suited him. Her courage almost failed her as the driver pointed the nose of the car towards a helicopter parked on the tarmac of the small local airport, and bringing it to a halt he stuck his head out of the window and called to a man waiting beside the machine,

'Here's your passenger, Jim.' He seemed to know the man, and the errand she was on. Probably whoever had called him up from the rig had explained the urgency of it. At least the oil people were efficient, Margaret conceded reluctantly, and tried to stifle the prick of resentment that still lurked from when she picked up her case at the hospital, and turned to see a hire car driver coming through her office door.

'Someone radioed for me to collect a doctor, and take him to the air-strip?'

They were so sure that they could have just what they wanted, the moment they wanted it. . . . She ought to be grateful for the quick organisation, it had saved her a lot of time, but——

'I'm a her, not a him, and I'm ready, so let's go,' she retorted with some asperity, which misfired completely on her driver, for he handed her into the front passenger seat beside him, gave her a merry look, and offered unabashed,

'If our family doctor looked like you, I'd go sick a lot more often than I do!'

His cheerful flow of chatter lightened her mood a little, until they reached the small, bleak air-strip that served the locality and the outlying islands.

'Who's he?' Sudden apprehension made her blunt, and she gazed at the figure waiting beside the helicopter with a conscious tightening of her throat.

'He's the pilot.' Her driver helped her out of the car and handed her her case. 'Don't worry, though,' he grinned as the man turned, and came towards them, 'he looks a lot younger than he is. He's quite a good pilot, really.'

Margaret did not care what he looked like. Even, at the moment, what sort of pilot he was. So long as he did not possess flaxen hair and gentian blue eyes....

'Don't let that lot down there worry you,' the pilot called Jim told her now, indicating the seemingly endless expanse of wild-looking sea with a casual wave of his hand. 'She's capable of coping with a lot worse weather than this.' He spoke of his machine with almost paternal pride. 'You get good visibility from her, don't you?' He fished for compliments for his beloved helicopter.

Margaret looked down, and for a second or two she closed her eyes. The visibility was a lot too good, so far as she was concerned, she thought, with a sick feeling inside her. She would have preferred to see a lot less water and a lot more land; preferably, feel the land firm beneath her own two feet.

'I didn't think helicopters were so big.' She tried to steady her shaky nerves by conversation. They were heading out towards the oil rig at a fast rate. Towards the rig, and in all probability, towards Dom. She tried to tell herself that the tight knot in her stomach was caused by the storm—by the strange mode of transport. . . .

'The Chinook's a heavy duty machine,' the pilot looked pleased at her unexpected interest. 'It doubles as personnel and load carrier, and it's got a long range, too,' he informed her proudly.

Margaret only half heard his enthusiastic description. Her anxious eyes caught what seemed to be a small, stable black patch in the middle of the heaving sea, some way in front of them. She caught sight of another, a little way further off. They might be ships, of course, nothing to do with the oil rig.

'There's the rig, look,' the pilot shattered her hope. 'In front of us. That dark patch over there,' he pointed.

'There are two of them.' To her untutored eyes, both dark patches looked alike from this distance.

'The one to our left is the rig. The other one's the stand-by vessel.'

'Standing by for what?' She did not really care, but talking helped to calm her now screaming nerves.

'It's got workshop and fire-fighting facilities and so on. And of course in an emergency it could evacuate the rig,' the pilot answered her laconically.

'Is the hospital on the ship?' Sudden hope flared in her. Dom would be on the rig itself, not the ship. She might not have to face him after all.

'The ship's got its own sick bay, of course, but the hospital's on the rig,' the pilot destroyed her last hope and pointed downwards, unconscious of the despair his words had caused. 'That's the rig coming up now, look.'

'There isn't much of it.' Margaret regarded the rapidly approaching structure with growing trepidation, and a curious kind of compassion. It looked tiny, and desperately lonely, set in the middle of the wild water, isolated and alien between the vast expanse of sea and sky, and out of sight of land. Out of touch with all human contact except by radio-telephone, whose cry for help had brought her here. Her resentment at the journey died within her.

'The rig's a semi-submersible,' the pilot told her casually, and so far as Margaret was concerned, incomprehensibly. 'There's a lot more of it under the water than shows on top.'

'There seems to be very little showing on top.' She swallowed with a throat that had suddenly become dry. 'Most of it seems to be that pylon thing, sticking up at the side,' she indicated a high tapering steel structure, at whose use she could not even begin to guess. 'We surely can't land on that?' Her eyes went wide with apprehension.

'That pylon thing, as you call it, is the derrick mast,' the pilot laughed at her obvious nervousness. 'Relax, lady, we don't land on that. The helicopter deck is that raised, flat octagonal area at the opposite corner of the rig. We go round the derrick to get to it.'

His explanation was meant to be reassuring, but failed signally. The raised, flat, octagonal area looked to be about as big as a pocket handkerchief, but there seemed to be nowhere else on the rig available for them to land. Peering down, Margaret saw that the rest of the square structure sticking out of the sea seemed to be cluttered with such a miscellany of equipment and sub-structures that there scarcely seemed room for a toy helicopter to land, let alone the one bearing them down towards it now. It had got to be the pocket handkerchief. . . .

'Isn't there a danger you'll miss it, in this wind?' she ventured. She had heard of aircraft ditching in the sea, and nothing but fish could possibly keep afloat in such wild water.

'I'll counter any drift,' the man at the controls told her with a sublime confidence she wished fervently she could share. 'Here we go. They'll be right glad to see you,' he told her warmly.

'Not half as glad as I shall be to see them,' she said sincerely, 'and for an entirely different reason,' she added silently to herself, and resisted the temptation to shut her eyes again as the helicopter circled round the derrick mast, hovered for a moment, then began to descend on the much too small-looking deck.

Ant-like figures appeared below them. The octagonal landing patch became progressively and reassuringly bigger, but Margaret was suddenly not interested in its size any longer. How or where they landed became irrelevant beside the crowd of men appearing below them. Her eyes sharpened, and she scanned the upturned faces with a quickened heartbeat. One or two of the men, despite the storm, were bareheaded, scorning protection from the elements. One, like herself, owned a shock of red hair. She smiled, in spite of her tension. His head stuck out like a beacon, guiding them in. Next to him—her smile faded—next to him stood a man with hair that was short, and flaxen-fair.

The rest of the little crowd surged forward as the helicopter got lower, but he stood still, his face upraised, unmoving. They were not quite low enough yet for her to see the colour of his eyes, but she knew already, she did not need to look. They would be a vivid gentian blue. She drew in a hard breath and her heart began to thud uncomfortably.

'There you are, smack on target! I told you not to worry.' The young pilot turned to her with a grin. 'Give me your case, I'll carry it down for you.' His voice, the touch of his hand on her own as he grasped her to help her down from the machine, jolted Margaret back to the reason for her mission. Willing hands helped steady her on to the deck of the rig, took her bag from the pilot, and turned to help him lash his machine safely. They parted away from Margaret, going about their various tasks, and for the first time she stood clearly in Dom's view.

She looked straight across at him, and his head turned towards her. He started, stared, and galvanised into action. In three quick strides he stood by her side.

'What on earth are you doing here?' He gripped her arm with fingers of steel. He looked furiously angry.

'I/C Vessel sent ashore for a doctor, Mr Orr,' a voice
spoke up from among the men still left disengaged. 'Our
own doc took a tumble in the storm last night.'

'I'm aware of that,' Dom cut short the other's explanation curtly. 'That was no reason for you to come out
here,' he snapped at Margaret.

'You wanted a doctor—you've got one. I'm a doctor,' she
reminded him sharply. Her own anger rose to meet his.
All the pent-up nervous tension of the day, culminating
in the palpitating experience of the flight, suddenly crystallised into fury at his unreasonable attitude. He had no
right. . . .

'So far as I'm concerned, you're a woman,' he flung
back at her harshly. 'And an oil rig in the middle of a gale
is no place for a woman. You're going back.'

'I'm doing no such thing!' She twisted round to face
him, her eyes blazing. 'I intend to do what I came here for,'
she gritted through clenched teeth. 'I'm going to attend to
whoever's been injured, and if necessary take them back
with me to the shore hospital. And until I've done that,
I'll stay right here where I am, gale or no gale,' she flung at
him. It was a pity she had to fling her words upwards.
Although she was wearing shoes, they were flat-heeled,
pump-soled, suitable for ward work, but doing little to add
to her height or her self-confidence.

Dom glared down at her, his eyes implacably hostile—
as if I'm invading taboo territory over which he has the
sole control, she thought incredulously.

'I'd better go and fetch I/C Vessel.'

One part of her mind caught the embarrassed mutter
of the man who held her case. Registered it, and then dismissed it. She neither knew nor cared who I/C Vessel was.
The oil people seemed to use a terminology of their own.
She disregarded the fact that so did the medical profession.
She was in no mood to be fair, least of all to anyone con-
nected with the rig. If I/C Vessel was a human being, which
she was beginning to doubt, he was probably another of the

tin god variety, who expected his lightest whim to be instantly obeyed, the same as Dom, she thought witheringly.

'Try your caveman tactics on someone else!' she shouted at him above the wind. She had to shout, to make her voice heard above the gusts. She resented Dom's hold on her, but on the exposed deck of the rig it was difficult to stand without it. 'They won't work on me,' she cried defiantly. She twisted her arm, trying ineffectually to free herself from his grasp, and never mind whether she could stand against the storm or not.

'I just might do that, if you don't go back on the helicopter with your patients,' he growled warningly. He did not have to raise his voice, Margaret noticed, but she heard every word he said quite clearly. 'Do you understand?' His grip tightened, and he pulled her towards him, to make sure she heard what he said.

'I'll go back when I think fit, and not when you say so.' She struggled against his inexorable pull. The clasp of his fingers bit into her wrist, their grip hard, on the edge of pain.

'Let go of my arm! I came here to attend patients, not to be held a prisoner by you.' Her smarting wrist, the restriction of his hold, or perhaps it was just the nearness of him to her, made something snap, and she pushed against him with all her strength. Fury gave her arms twice their normal power and caught him unawares. He staggered back under the force of her push, his grip loosening slightly, although he did not quite let go.

'In future, keep your hands off ... oh, my watch!'

She swung her arm wildly, frantic to release herself from his hold, and the movement pulled the cuff of her sleeve clear of her wrist, exposing her watch.

Dom's fingers still held her loosely, and their wrists touched. The sleeve of his bulky-knit sweater snagged on the catch of her watch bracelet, and the two ends flew apart. Margaret grabbed at it, and so did Dom. Their hands collided, and missed the watch, and they looked on help-

lessly as it flashed a dull silver in the drab light and described an arc above them towards the side of the rig.

She turned away, stunned, unable to watch her precious
gift vanish in the green, heaving waters. Her eyes stung
suddenly, and she turned on the geologist furiously.

'Now I've lost my watch, and it's your fault,' she accused him wildly. 'Does it make you happy, that you've
lost me the only thing I really value?' she cried.

CHAPTER SEVEN

'Here's I/C Vessel coming up, doctor.'

A loud cough broke the tight silence between them, and
the man carrying her case reappeared, still with her case
in his hand. Margaret wished crossly that he would put
it down, and then realised he probably held on to it for
safety's sake, in case there was anything breakable inside.
She turned to meet the mysterious I/C Vessel, and got a
shock.

'I'm sorry to keep you waiting, doctor.' He stepped forward with his hand outstretched. 'Your local weather's a
bit inhospitable.' He smiled, taking the sting from his
criticism. 'It caused us one or two difficulties last night,'
he understated in a gentle voice. 'I'm the Offshore Installation Manager, in charge of the welfare of personnel on the
rig. It was I who sent for you,' he introduced himself.

'I/C Vessel—I know.' In spite of herself, Margaret
smiled. Whatever she had expected, it was not this, she told
herself disbelievingly. The newcomer proved to be round,
middle-aged and balding, with a pink and white complexion, and a harassed look, and would have seemed more
in place behind the counter of a local bank, or in a solici-
tor's office. On the rig, he seemed as out of place as she
was. The thought brought her a small crumb of comfort,

and a sense of fellowship that was distinctly lacking with Dom.

'I'll show you where our hospital is, if you'll follow me?'

He turned and led the way below, his mild manner and gentle, nodding invitation for her to use him as a guide, giving the impression that he was escorting her along quiet corridors to some hallowed inner office sanctum. A sense of unreality took possession of Margaret as she took in their wild surroundings. The skeletal derrick towering above them; the high, curling breakers; the white spume, and the shrieking gusts that took all her strength to stand against, and the deck of the rig beneath her feet wet with driven spray. She fought down a sense that she was not really there at all, that she must be dreaming, and turned to follow her guide.

She did not see if Dom came with them. She could hear footsteps behind her, but they might or might not belong to him. She resisted an almost overpowering impulse to turn round and look, then her guide stopped at a door in the corridor and she stood aside for him to open it, and she was able to turn naturally, without betraying curiosity. And there was only the man, carrying her case. Dom was nowhere to be seen.

Contrarily, she felt an instant of sickening let-down. Then her guide opened the door, and her own familiar world greeted her from inside it. The clinical smell of disinfectant, the equipment—her quickly probing eyes saw that despite the small scale of the miniature hospital, it seemed well equipped for emergencies.

'We've got two of almost everything, except doctors,' a tired-sounding voice from a nearby bunk informed her, and she turned to confront the reason for her being there.

'I'm the M.O. for the rig.' His face was grey, with the sweat of pain making it shiny, but he sounded rational enough.

'Are you the only casualty?' It seemed callous, but she had to know.

'No, there are two more, but fortunately I'd patched them up before I took a dive myself. They're walking wounded,' he explained faintly. 'Sprains and cuts, nothing serious.'

'What damage have you done to yourself?' She spoke briskly, sure of herself again, and with the added bonus of a patient who knew what he was talking about.

'Tib and fib gone. I heard them—and felt them.' He stifled a groan.

'What have you taken to ease the pain?'

'Nothing.' He saw her look of surprise and gave a crooked grin. 'I daren't, you see, in case anyone else got hurt in the blow last night, and I had to instruct someone what to do for them,' he said simply. 'I daren't risk losing consciousness....'

'Now I'm here, I'll take the responsibility.' Margaret hid both admiration and compassion and swiftly set about preparing a hypodermic.

'This won't hurt,' she murmured automatically, then, at his grimace, 'Sorry, I'd forgotten you were one of us.' She grinned along with him as she remembered who he was.

'Spare me the bedside manner,' he begged. 'Ooh, I hate those things!' He screwed up his face with the unashamed cowardice common among the profession who wield such instruments. 'Over to you,' he murmured drowsily a few minutes later, and relaxed with a long sigh of relief as the drug began to take hold.

Margaret lost count of time after that. Vaguely she was aware of the storm in the background. The effect of the mountainous, curling waves and screaming gusts of wind that battered the rig with monotonous, shuddering regularity. But here, in the tiny hospital bay, she had work to do, and that took precedence over everything. Her hair was damp against her forehead with the sustained effort. At the General, she had a team of helpers. Here, she was on her own. She, who had never owned any sea legs to speak of, found them now in the stress of dire need. Once the man who carried her case down for her put his head round the door and asked,

'Mr Orr said to ask you how long you'd be, Doc? Because of going back on the 'copter?'

'You can tell Dominic Orr I'll be as long as is necessary,' she retorted crisply. 'You can't put a patient away like a geology sample, until a more convenient time—he should have the sense to realise that.' Dom had no authority over her, or the rig hospital, and it was high time he was made to know it, she thought angrily. 'When I'm finished, I'll let the Offshore Installation Manager know,' she rubbed her point home and added, repenting slightly of her sharpness, after all it was not this man's fault she would not put up with the geologist's domineering ways, 'I need a hand to hold the patient's foot steady for me, while I use a plaster bandage,' she begged his help with a smile.

'I dunno, Doc.' Unexpectedly, he backed towards the door. 'I'd like well enough to help, but. . . .' He averted his eyes from what she was doing, and went several shades paler beneath his tan. 'I'll go and fetch someone,' he muttered, and vanished.

'Of all the. . . .' Margaret let out her breath in a rush of exasperation. 'Oh well,' she shrugged, 'I suppose it's no more that I should have expected.' Healthy young men, engaged on work that demanded the peak of physical fitness, were usually the first to succumb to nerves at the sight of illness or injury, and the means taken to treat it. She frowned. Now her bag carrier had defected, she was in a quandary. She dared not let go of her patient's foot, or else the broken bones would spring out of place again and cause worse injury. She could manage if she had to, but it would be easier with another pair of hands.

She paused for a moment to think, and rubbed her forehead against the top of her sleeve, wiping the dampness from her eyes. The sheer physical effort of the task she was engaged upon, added to the tensions of the evening

before, and then her brush with Dom on the deck, culminating in the loss of her watch—she did not want to
think about the loss of her watch—had drained her more
than she had realised.

'Tell me what you want done, and I'll do it.' He spoke
quietly, from just over her head.

'You!'

She nearly let go of her patient's foot with the sudden
shock of his voice so close to her. Convulsively she tightened her grip, lest she undo all the work she had already
done. She swallowed, and drew a deep, steadying breath,
forcing herself to speak normally.

'Put your one hand over the top of his foot—like this—
and the other under his heel, and hold it firmly. Don't
pull too hard.' Professional training came to her aid, and
with an effort that cost her almost the last of her remaining
strength she forced herself to remain calm and instruct
him what to do. 'When your hands are in position over
mine, I'll slide my own from under as you take over the
pressure.'

But even professional training could not subdue the
sudden clamour of her senses as his hands closed over her
own. The rising excitement within her, which she could
not quite control, provoked by his nearness, and accentuated by his touch.

'I'm hungry,' she told herself, trying to find a reason, an
excuse, trying to force her swimming head to concentrate
on the task in front of her. Bitterly she regretted her
snatched and scanty breakfast, the barely touched cheese
roll and coffee at lunch time. Lack of food did not help in
such circumstances, and it was not helping her now. She
tried to convince herself that it was hunger for food that
made her legs feel so weak. Not hunger for the man beside
her, to feel his arms round her, holding her close. To be
something special—not just like any other woman—to him.
She sighed sharply. It must be hours since she left the
hospital. It seemed like a lifetime. Automatically she glanced

at her watch, and her empty wrist brought back a rising flood of anger through her. A saving flood, because it brought back a temporary strength to her that nothing else could have done. She raised eyes that were suddenly hard. Dom must have seen her glance to where her watch had been, but he met her look with one as cool as her own was hostile.

'It's eighteen hundred hours,' he told her evenly, and added indifferently, 'Let's get on with this, shall we?' as if he was the one in charge, and she was the underling.

Margaret compressed her lips and got on with it. There was little else she could do. She dunked bandages and rolled them with savage concentration, trying to blot out the fact that he was there beside her. She worked in silence, and Dom did not offer to speak, and before she was half way through the tension stretched her nerves until they twanged like violin strings. Fervently she wished she was back at the General, where the silence was never like this, only the result of busy teamwork, holding none of the electric undercurrents of antagonism and awareness that flowed between herself and the geologist like a tangible presence, as obvious as the all-pervading clinical smell of the small sick bay.

Her own staff helped her with a common purpose. Dom, she suspected, merely lent a hand for the sole purpose of speeding her return to the mainland at the earliest possible moment. The pilot's welcoming, 'They'll be glad to see you,' did not include Dom, she thought bitterly.

'You can let go now. It'll hold.'

She spoke flatly. She did not add, 'Thank you.' What Dom had done was to serve his own purpose, not to help her; so she had nothing to thank him for. She turned away from him with a dismissive gesture and began to soap her hands and arms at the sink. Perhaps when she turned back again he would be gone. She soaped them twice, then dried them with meticulous care, to give him time to register her lack of welcome, but either he could not read the signs, or he read them and chose to ignore them. Probably the latter. I should have known better, she thought wearily, and laid the towel down with a defeated shrug and turned back towards the bunk.

It could have been the storm, or weariness, or hunger— either sort of hunger—that caused her to sway. She grasped at the bunk rail for support and held on grimly.

'It's time you finished, you've about had enough.' Dom's voice was rough behind her.

'I'll finish when my patient's made comfortable, and not before.' She spoke quietly, over her shoulder, not deigning to turn her head. To her relief, he did not argue. Something in her tone, or manner, must have convinced him.

'I haven't got my sea legs yet,' she offered what excuse she could, if only to prevent him from speaking first, to bring up any objections. 'I'll press up against the bunk rail, it'll steady me long enough to tidy him up.'

'Whereabouts do you want to stand?'

'Where I am now. Why?' She looked up and back at him now, registering her surprise at his question.

'In that case, I'll hold you.'

He did not wait for her to say yes or no. He stepped up behind her, not crowding her, but leaving her plenty of room to move freely and attend to her patient, although pressing enough for her to feel him touch against her, making a backing for her to lean against if she needed it. He reached out a hand and grasped the bunk rail on one side of her; reached out another, and did the same, so that his hold surrounded her.

'You can lean back against me, if it helps.'

He must be in a hurry to get rid of me, she thought with a cynical downcurving of her lips, but nevertheless she felt glad of his support as she attended to her patient. Once, twice, she would have lost her footing on the unstable deck if it had not been for the ramrod firmness of his arms, which remained unmoving, his hands gripping the rails

on either side of her as he withstood her unsteady weight
with effortless ease.

Finally she gave the still unconscious M.O. a last check,
tucked the blankets round him—and suddenly went limp
herself. Now the necessity for action was ended, a wave of
utter tiredness swept over her. The battering fury of the
storm pounded even louder against her consciousness, more
insistent than before, probably because she had nothing
to occupy her, she supposed. She leaned back wearily, and
started violently as she felt a hard warmth against her. For
the moment, she had forgotten.... She straightened, and
rubbed a hand across her eyes dazedly. Dom's hands were
still linked over the bunk rail, one on each side of her, supporting her—or holding her in? She glanced up at him
swiftly, uncertainly, and her temper rose at the amused
curve on his lips.

'I've finished now.' She spoke sharply, on the edge of
sudden fear.

'But I haven't.' Unhurriedly he loosened his fingers
from the bunk rail, but instead of dropping his arms to his
side and releasing her, he transferred his hands to her
waist, and turned her to face him. 'In fact, I've only just
started,' he told her grimly. Margaret raised startled eyes to
his face, his jaw square above her, with the hard inflexibil-
ity of granite.

'Let me go....' His lips stopped her words. They
clamped hard on her mouth, silencing her, blotting out
her weariness and the sound of the storm. Blotting out
everything but the wild pounding of blood in her ears.
Punishing her for coming to the rig in the first place; for
blaming him for the loss of her watch. Challenging her to
a response that she willed herself not to give.

'That's something for you to remember your great adventure by.' He released her at last, and she dropped, panting,
away from him, and leaned weakly against the edge of
the bunk, fighting for breath.

'How dare you suggest....' she began furiously.

'Well, isn't that what this is, to you?' He cut across her outburst with a cold incisiveness. 'Woman doctor, braving gale to succour oil rig? It should look great as headlines in your local newspaper,' he jeered sarcastically. 'Isn't that what you had in mind—glory-seeking?'

'It was nothing of the kind!'

White-hot fury stiffened her away from the bunk rail, giving her strength to stand on her own. 'Bill had to....' She started to tell him that Bill had had to remain in theatre when she left. That she herself did not want to come, but dared not delay answering the call in case it might be urgent. In case someone's life might depend upon her speed. Then she stopped, biting the words back. Why should she offer any explanation to this arrogant, self-opinionated creature? she asked herself stormily. He did not send for her to come. He was not even in charge of the welfare of personnel on the rig. And he had no right to an explanation of the reason for her decision to come out herself.

Let him think what he likes! she thought mutinously. It would probably be the worst, anyway, she decided bitingly and pressed her lips together, forcing the words back. Lips that still felt numb from the pressure he had put upon them, tingling with a hunger that was not for food. A hunger that might have broken her will, making her give in to his challenge, if he had not stopped when he did.

'So Bill Quinn had to stay meekly behind, because you said so?' He drew his own conclusions from her silence. 'Because you're in charge at the General, while your chief is away? I wonder who Neil Venables would have sent, if he'd been there?' His tone said he already knew the answer. So did Margaret herself, but Neil had not been there, and there had been no other course open to her. If there had, she would have taken it—anything rather than come out to the rig herself. But Dom was not to know that, and she did not intend to explain. 'If that's Women's Lib,' his voice was brittle, 'spare me from it,' he said forcefully.

'If Women's Lib means being spared arrogant, domineering, bullying behaviour, then I'm all for it,' she flashed back, careless of the fact that until now she had not given it —or anything else, for that matter—very much thought. She had been far too absorbed in her work. 'And as for glory-seeking,' she flung back at him angrily, 'so far as I'm concerned, all that I've got out of this trip is a nerve-racking air flight, a lot of hard work, and a lost watch.' Her voice wavered on the last, despite her determination to keep it steady.

'The loss of your watch is your own fault.'

'My fault?' She glared at him furiously. 'How can you say it's my fault, when you. . . .'

'You knew the fastening was unsafe. You shouldn't have worn it again until it was mended,' he thrust back remorselessly. 'Particularly on a place like an oil rig,' he emphasised his objection to her being there.

'I shan't be on the rig for much longer.' Sudden tears stung the back of her eyes. Tears of futile anger, and equally futile longing—she would not let herself think for what. 'My patient's fit to travel, and I'll contact I/C Vessel and tell him I'm ready to go. Glad to go.' She choked into silence and turned blindly back towards the bunk.

'I'm afraid you'll have to put up with our hospitality for a little longer, Doctor Warrender.' A pink and white face below a balding head surveyed her apologetically from the doorway. 'Unless it's a matter of life and death that your patient is taken ashore?' I/C Vessel diplomatically left the decision to her.

'Goodness, no, he's only got a broken leg, and that's been set. Your M.O.'s perfectly fit otherwise.'

'In that case, I'm afraid you'll have to remain as our guest for a little longer, until the storm subsides.'

'It's essential that Doctor Warrender goes ashore now.' Dom turned on the man angrily. 'Her hospital is desperately short-handed—or so I was led to believe.' His glance seared her, questioning the veracity of her earlier complaint.

'That doesn't justify me sending anyone back in a blow like this,' the Offshore Installation Manager interrupted Margaret's angry rejoinder.

'If the pilot won't take the Chinook up, I will.'

'No one will take the helicopter up, Mr Orr.' Beneath the deceptively gentle manner there lay steel, Margaret perceived gleefully. 'The storm's running up to Force Ten. I would only allow the 'copter to take off in the case of a dire emergency. And Doctor Warrender says there is no emergency,' he finished with an air of finality.

So it was not merely lack of occupation that had made the storm seem so much worse, she realised. It really was. But at least her judgment had been accepted, in preference to Dom's. She shot the geologist a triumphant glance. So much for his arrogant high-handedness! She tilted her head and looked up at him, and flushed as she met the condemnation in his narrowed eyes.

'Glory-seeking,' the blue gaze flicked at her accusingly.

Her chin came up defiantly. Let him think what he pleased! She would have sent Bill out to the rig if she could, but Dom did not know that, and she did not intend to explain her actions to him.

'By the way,' the thought of Bill made her remember the difficulties at the General, 'can you radio ashore and let them know what's happening?'

'Of course,' the middle-aged man spoke mildly, as if it was merely a matter of popping along the street, and Margaret marvelled afresh at his calm acceptance of the, to her, bizzare surroundings. 'I wanted to ask if you'd like any particular message transmitted?'

'Yes, please.' She turned to her questioner thankfully. At least while she was talking to him she had to keep her mind on practical matters, which helped her for the moment at least to ignore Dom, even if she could not quite forget his glowering presence behind her. 'Tell them I'll be back with a fracture case the very moment it's possible to make the flight.' She emphasised 'the very moment'. Dom must not be allowed to think she enjoyed the prospect of an enforced stay on the rig, that she enjoyed being here at all. She would be as glad to leave as he would be to see her go. 'Oh, and ask if Doctor Ralph Rollason,' she repeated the name so that he should not forget it, 'would be kind enough to continue to stand in for me until I return. I had to co-opt his help in a hurry, when your call came,' she explained with a smile. And Dom could make what he liked of that, too, she thought defiantly.

'I'll attend to it for you,' I/C Vessel promised, and added, 'and find some suitable accommodation for you for the night, as well.'

'She can have my cabin,' Dom said evenly.

'I wouldn't dream of putting you out,' Margaret refused instantly.

'We're not in the habit of allowing people to sleep on deck,' he told her coldly, and turned to the other man. 'I was sharing the M.O.'s cabin anyway, because I'm officially on leave, and the cabin Lex and I usually share is occupied by our opposite numbers on duty,' he explained. 'If I occupy the other bunk here in the sick bay, it'll leave the M.O.'s cabin free, and I can keep an eye on him during the night in case he wakes up and wants something.'

It sounded an ideal arrangement, on the face of it. Margaret turned on him furiously.

'If the M.O. needs help, I'm to be called,' she cried angrily. She hated him for his cool disposal of her person, and the equally cool usurping of her authority over her patient.

'If he needs medical help, naturally you'll be called.' He dismissed her protest casually, as one would brush away an irritating fly. It was like hammering against a locked door. She felt the now familiar sense of impotent fury choke the words that rose to her lips.

'That will be most convenient.' The other man's pedantic

manner began to get on her nerves, but before she could say anything he went on, 'If you can leave your patient now, and come with me, I'll show you where you'll sleep. And you must be hungry too, by now,' he smiled.

'Do we have to cross the deck again?' For a moment, apprehension took hold and drove away any hunger pangs she might have. If it was unsafe for the immensely strong-looking helicopter to take off.... Unconsciously her eyes sought Dom's face, and surprised a strange expression there. Perhaps she only imagined it, because the next second it was gone, and his expression was stern and set, as she was used to it. Or maybe he was simply gloating over her nervousness, glad that she was afraid, and using her fear as a bludgeon to punish her for her temerity in invading this male dominated world of his. The thought stiffened her courage. She would brave any gale rather than show weakness in front of Dom.

'We stay below decks,' her guide reassured her, and in spite of herself a small sigh of relief escaped her. 'We don't want you swept overboard,' he added with a smile, 'that would be poor recompense for your coming to our aid.'

Margaret smiled back at him brightly, glad of the chance to smile, though it did not seem like a particularly good joke to her. But at least it showed Dom she did not care, either for the storm or for him. And it helped to hide her chagrin when, as she turned to quit the sick bay after her guide, the geologist had the silent, last word, by remaining behind. Occupying—and by implication, in charge of—what was by right her sole domain.

CHAPTER EIGHT

Now she was occupying Dom's domain.

She surveyed the compact cabin with grudging approval. There did not seem to be an inch of wasted space anywhere, and the small, domestic corner of her heart that even her interest in her profession could not quite deny marvelled at the skill that amounted to genius which designed the fittings to give the utmost storage capacity, and yet still managed to avoid any impression that the accommodation was cramped, even for two men.

'I'll have this bunk made up for you,' her guide promised, 'but you can leave your case here if you like while you freshen up, then I'll come back for you in a little while and take you to dinner. Say ten minutes?'

Margaret nodded, and automatically again looked for her watch. And again found it missing, and a surge of anger returned at the cause of her loss. She dumped her case on a locker top with unnecessary force and promptly grabbed at it as it slid.

'It's better if you put it inside the locker,' her companion advised her. 'It's only small, it'll just about fit in.' He fitted it in for her, in company with another, much larger case, and a smaller holdall. 'We put everything away in a blow like this, it saves breakages,' he said simply, and Margaret nodded. It explained the barren appearance of the cabin.

'Ten minutes, then?' The door closed behind him, and she sat down on the bunk which he said would be prepared for her. Dom's bunk? Something told her that it was. She sank back on it, forcing herself to relax, letting her eyes roam over the small cabin. This was Dom's world. This, and the raw, elemental fury that roared and battered above them, venting its anger against those who dared to invade it in their search for what the geologist called black gold.

Deliberately she allowed her mind to dwell on Dom, guarded against him, for the moment anyway, by the anger that rode her, which gave her an armour of detachment of greater efficacy even than her white coat. He was a creature of strange contrasts. One minute he could be almost poetically descriptive about his work; the next, as hard as the rocks that provided him with his profession. She had evidence that he could be thoughtful. Had he not carried her coffee to the fire for her, at the supper party on Sunday evening? And then helped her to fasten her watch bracelet afterwards?

And this was where he returned to after he saw her home. The bunk she sat on now, was the one where he took his rest last night. And dreamed of what? Or whom? Of herself? It was doubtful. Her lips took on a wry twist. Dom travelled alone, without encumbrances, he had said as much himself. It would matter nothing to him that his kisses destroyed her own rest, her peace of mind. He would regard it as her own fault, like the loss of her watch.

She jumped to her feet restlessly. Her detachment was not proof against the intrusion of thoughts like this. Already she could feel herself begin to tremble. She started and spun round as footsteps sounded outside the door, but they passed on. She heard another door close, further along the corridor, and hurriedly set about tidying herself up. I/C Vessel said ten minutes, and she had no means of knowing how many of those minutes had already ticked by. She pulled a hurried comb through her hair and patted it into place just as a discreet knock sounded on her own door.

'I see you're ready.' He smiled his approval of what he saw, and Margaret's spirits lifted. I/C Vessel's frank admiration boosted her morale as nothing else could have done at the moment, and already she felt better. Food, however basic, would complete the cure, she told herself staunchly.

'Mr Orr and the helicopter pilot are joining us for the meal,' her guide told her, and destroyed her appetite at a stroke. 'I thought it might be nice for you to have your meal with two people you know,' he added with kindly consideration.

'Er—yes.' She agreed about the pilot, but not about Dom. With an effort, she stopped herself from saying so. She would sit out the meal with what fortitude she could muster, she decided, and excuse herself on the grounds of tiredness as soon as possible afterwards. She could go to her cabin—Dom's cabin—she would have to eat something first. She was becoming confused. Hunger was making her lightheaded.

'This is the mess.' His words prepared her for stark, barrack-like conditions, which she had unconsciously expected on the rig. They did not prepare her for the tastefully furnished comfort into which she followed him. Dom and the pilot sat waiting for them at a table near the door, and they both rose to their feet as she approached. The pilot pulled back a chair for her with pleased gallantry, and Margaret saw Dom frown. It could not be that he was jealous. That was impossible, she told herself incredulously. It was just that he liked to be in the forefront of everything himself. She made her smile sweeter than she would otherwise have done, and murmured her thanks to the pilot as she sat down, with suddenly racing heart. Had Dom taken his chair knowing he would be sitting opposite to her, across the table? That each time she looked up she must encounter his eyes? She did not put it past him. He would lose no opportunity to press home his disapproval of her presence on the rig.

'It's an unusual occasion, we've never had the opportunity to entertain a lady guest on the rig before,' the pilot smiled his satisfaction at the arrangement, and Dom's scowl grew black.

'Let's hope it's a unique occasion,' he growled ungraciously, and Margaret flushed. Need he be quite so blunt? she wondered angrily. Particularly in front of the others? But before she could think of a suitable reply another voice joined in.

'I got the message through to the shore hospital, Chief.' A man approached the table and spoke to the Offshore Installation Manager, though his eyes strayed with open appreciation of Margaret, a fact which deepened Dom's scowl and brightened Margaret's smile with a brightness that was beginning to fade with her appetite, she thought wretchedly. The newcomer seemed to be a radio operator of some sort.

'Was there any message back?' his Chief asked.

'Only one, for you, Doctor,' he turned to Margaret. 'It was from a Doctor Quinn.' His eyes twinkled with friendly laughter. 'He says to mind your teeth on the ship's biscuit, miss—ma'am. . . .' He gave up the unequal struggle to determine which was correct, grinned engagingly, and withdrew, and Margaret chuckled, her tension released.

'There's not much connection with ship's biscuit here.'

The meal was superb. It easily outclassed many a meal she had eaten in a starred hotel. And it had been prepared and served in the middle of a gale.

'It's amazing!' She voiced her frank admiration. 'Do you always eat in this style?' It could not be a meal put on specially for her benefit, they did not know she was coming, and it was generally expected that the visiting doctor would go back the same day in the helicopter with the patient. She would be gone now, if Dom had had his way, in spite of the risks. She glanced up at him, found he was watching her, and hurriedly looked away again.

'Indeed we do.' The Offshore Installation Manager leaned back in his chair and looked at her with open amusement. 'There have even been critics of our style of living on the oil rigs. Some say it's far too high.'

'You can't take men of the calibre this industry demands, dump them in the middle of some of the most inhospitable places on the globe, and expect them to withstand the rigours of the work and the climate on poor food,' Dom interrupted flatly from the other side of the table, and Margaret compressed her lips. He spoke as if it was she who had done the criticising. She bit back an angry retort as the other man continued,

'I think perhaps you *did* expect something like ship's biscuit?' he teased, and her lips released themselves in an upward curve.

'Perhaps something more in the bacon and beans line,' she confessed, 'certainly not anything as good as this.'

'The recreational facilities are pretty comprehensive, too.' He was obviously longing to boast about the rig, and Margaret rose from her chair. She had to pass the time somehow before she could reasonably escape to her cabin, and anything was better than sitting facing Dom's angry glare.

'If the weather was a bit calmer, we could offer you a game of table tennis, or a cinema show, but I think in a blow like this it might be better to settle for the reading room.'

Her sense of unreality grew as she followed her guide. If it had not been for the constant movement she might have been walking through the rooms of any good class hotel. The reading room greeted her with bright hangings and a warmly carpeted floor—or did they call it a deck? Comfortable chairs, with tables for those who wished to write, were scattered about the room, which was well occupied. A stir of interest greeted her arrival, and after a moment of surprised silence, a murmur of polite 'good evenings', and then the occupants resumed their various occupations. She noticed an atmosphere of interested busyness pervaded the place, and glanced across at her escort with raised eyebrows.

'A number of the rig staff are studying for extra degrees,' he responded willingly. 'The sort of shifts we work provide ideal conditions for study.'

'Lex Noble told me you work a fortnight about,' Margaret prompted him, eager to keep him talking. Dom had not followed them into the reading room, and her eyes strayed to the door. Would he come and join them? Or was he only too glad that I/C Vessel had taken over as host, and so rid him of an unwelcome feeling of responsibility for her while she was on the rig? Talking helped to gloss over the empty desolation inside her, that told her the latter was probably true.

'The crew work twelve-hour shifts.' He seemed not to

notice her distraction, and cantered along on his hobbyhorse happily enough. 'Allowing for eating and sleeping, it usually leaves a few clear hours a day for those who want to study. We've even got some language classes going,' he said proudly. 'Each national teaches his own tongue, and in turn learns another. It broadens the individual's scope, and helps weld the crew together. A common interest in their out-of-work hours could be difficult to find, otherwise.'

'I've noticed you've got a multi-national staff.' The roustabout was definitely an Australian; the pilot who brought her here was American; Lex hailed from Jamaica, and Dom from England. And the man who carried her bag down to the sick bay for her answered to a name that sounded Norwegian. She smiled. Her present companion was obviously a Scot.

'That's another thing that makes this such a fascinating trade.'

His north-of-the-Border burr droned on. The room was warm, the chair was soft and comfortable. A yawn caught Margaret unawares.

'There now, I'm keeping you talking, and you tired with the day you've had,' he exclaimed remorsefully. 'You'll be wanting your bed, no doubt.'

'I'd like to check on my patient first. Don't get up, I can find my own way easily enough.' Now she had got her bearings, the layout below deck was simple.

'I'll see you to the sick bay door, just the same,' he insisted in his quiet way, and she smiled as they reached the sick bay.

'You see, I could have found it easily enough.' He was a fusspot, but a nice one, she decided as she went inside, and discovered her patient propped up in his bunk, deep in a magazine.

'Hang-gliding!' she exclaimed. 'Isn't one broken leg enough for you, without reading up on a dangerous sport like that? It's worse than motor-cycling. And besides, you ought to be still asleep,' she told him severely.

'Hang-gliding's great,' his eyes shone with enthusiasm, 'and the country around here is ideal for it. All those hills!' He waved a happy hand. 'I hope we strike oil and stay here for ever.' He heaved himself upright in the bunk. Sleep looked to be the last thing on his mind, and Margaret smiled despite herself, relieved at his clear colour and quick recuperation from his ordeal.

'Just the same. . . .' she began doubtfully.

'Oh, have a heart,' he begged. 'The leg's fine, I should know if it wasn't. And reading helps me forget about it.'

'I shouldn't listen to your blarney.'

'But you will,' he grinned confidently, and picked up his magazine again.

'Don't take any risks, then,' she warned him. 'I don't want to have to do my work all over again.'

'You won't,' he assured her, and with that she had to be content. It was a relief to find him capable of coping for himself, and an equal relief to reach her cabin and to be on her own at last. She kicked off her shoes. She didn't have any nightclothes with her, she had not thought she would need them, but she could sleep in her slip. She folded her skirt and placed it on the top of the locker. It would not matter if it slid off during the night, there was nothing to break. She pulled her sweater over her head and folded it on the top of the skirt. The high neckline ruffled her hair as it came over her head, bubbling her curls round her face in tiny rings that made her look much younger than she really was, an impression enhanced by her slight figure and dainty white lace slip, that nevertheless covered the softly rounded contours of a woman. It was thus Dom saw her when he came in.

'What the blazes. . . !' He closed the door, turned round, and stood still, staring at her. 'What are you doing in here?' he demanded harshly.

'You said I could use your cabin.' She stammered to a halt under his furious glare. Her eyes, wide with shocked consternation, searched his face. If only she had kept her sweater on for just those few seconds longer! If only.... But Dom stood between her and her sweater, and although the cabin gave the impression of spaciousness, it was only an impression. The space did not really exist.

Her hands rose nervously, but they gave her inadequate cover, and desperately she regretted buying the opera-topped slip that was nearly all lace, instead of the much higher, straight-topped one that she had been shown for choice. Even the lace in the one she was wearing was reveal-ing. A hot tide of total embarrassment flooded across her throat and face. If only he would stop looking at her like that, as if—as if——

'Why didn't you remain in the sick bay until someone came for you?' His voice grated, flicking a nerve that re-stored her failing courage sufficiently to answer him.

'I can find my own way about well enough, it's quite simple. I don't need an escort everywhere I go.'

'In the shore hospital, probably not, but the same doesn't apply here,' he snapped. 'You're the only woman on the rig, among eighty men....'

'I've met a lot of them, and they're perfectly nice people,' she began indignantly. How dared he suggest....

'Oh, grow up!' he bade her savagely. 'Have you no con-ception what you do to a man—any man—looking as you do now?' He took her roughly by the shoulders, her bare, soft shoulders, that winced under the force of his grip and carried the clear marks of his fingers for the whole of the next day. 'Look at yourself,' he commanded, and turned her to face the mirror glass that was screwed to the wall—or was it the bulkhead, on an oil rig? 'Look at yourself.' He gave her a shake. 'Try to realise the risk you're taking. You're a doctor, you can't be that naïve.'

'If you hadn't barged in here without knocking, you wouldn't have seen me looking as I do now,' she blazed, and twisted round to face him, turning her back on the mirror and the truth she saw there. Turning her back on the reflection that was too close to her own for her comfort, of flaxen hair, and a pair of smouldering blue eyes that burned with a fire that threatened to set her alight, too. She sought refuge in anger.

'You shouldn't have come into the cabin at all. You'd no right.' Temper made her forget her embarrassment. She was as well covered as if she had been in evening dress, she told herself robustly, better covered than if she had worn a swimsuit.

'It's my cabin, I've got every right to come in. I/C Vessel told me you'd gone to the sick bay to check on the M.O., so I came to collect my things from the locker while you were supposed to be out.'

How like a man, to put the responsibility on her for his own thoughtless action! she thought furiously.

'Then take your things, and get out!' She spat the words at him and rushed on, for fear that if she stopped she might begin to listen to the sweet, wild music that sang through her veins again, orchestrated by the hard, warm grip on her shoulders that hurt with an ecstasy of pain she would rather bear than the cause should be removed. She clenched her teeth against the pain of it, and shut her ears to the music.

'Don't forget anything, and then find you have to come back for it.' Recklessly she flung at him the suggestion that he might do so deliberately.

'.... have you no conception what you do to a man—any man....' Did he include himself among them? she wondered. The thought caught at her throat with sudden fear.

'Or do I have to pay rent on the cabin, to ensure privacy?' She rushed on, burying the fear in words, as well as the music.

'You can pay for it in advance, my little wildcat,' he gritted, 'then perhaps you'll learn that your claws aren't such a wonderful protection as they might seem. Perhaps then you'll heed what I tell you.'

He pulled her to him. She fought, but she was no match for his superior strength. She opened her mouth to call out, and he closed it with his lips, blotting out the sound. She hammered balled fists against his chest, but she might as well have pitted her puny strength against the side of the oil rig itself, for all the impression she made.

After what seemed a long time the hammering ceased, and she made no attempt to call out when Dom's lips left her own, and trailed bands of searing fire along her throat and neck and across the softness of her shoulders to where his hands still held her, not allowing her to move. Then they trailed back again, exploring, caressing, with a deadly expertise that deliberately sought to arouse her response. It terrified her by its unexpected force when it came. She quivered under his touch, and went still. She could not resist him any longer. Her anger vanished as if it had never been, and the aching hunger came back. The hunger that was not for food, but for Dom—Dom—Dom——

She breathed his name, but she did not know whether she whispered it out loud, or not. She raised her head, and her eyes were wide with a passionate longing, soft with the memory of his other kisses, and begging for more.

He put her from him. His eyes burned black with a smouldering intensity that kindled a matching response from her newly awakened senses. She raised her hands to touch his face, to draw his head down again to meet her eager, parted lips. For a second the flaxen head began to bend again to her touch. Then it jerked backwards, and his eyes changed, hardened, grew remote and cold, as only blue eyes filled with contempt can grow cold. Margaret drew back, nonplussed.

'Dom?' She faltered to a halt.

'So even a wildcat will purr when it's stroked,' he sneered, taunting her with her own reaction. 'Perhaps now you'll see what I meant.'

She flinched as if he had struck her. So that was why he had kissed her! To show her, to teach her a lesson. Not because he wanted to, himself. She felt the cabin spin in a dizzy arc around her.

'But—but you. . . .'

'I kissed you?' He gave a short, harsh laugh. 'What did you expect me to do? I'm not a monk. Be thankful it was only a kiss.' He spun on his heel and reached the door with one angry stride. He turned there, and sent a last parting shot back at her as she stood numbly where he had left her. 'When I go out, lock the door behind me, and keep it that way until daylight,' he commanded her savagely, and slammed it with a force that felt as if it must surely shake the rig itself to its very foundations.

Margaret made no move to obey him immediately. She remained where she was, stunned into immobility as much by the knowledge that exploded on her consciousness with the brilliance of a meteorite as by the pain at his cavalier treatment.

'I love you! Dom, I love you. . . .'

Her voice came muffled through cold palms pressed against her bruised lips, and slow tears found their way across her fingertips and trickled down the backs of her hands. She did not want to love him. What was the use of loving a man who regarded women as encumbrances— something that got in the way of his work? It was hopeless, and she knew it, and the tears flowed faster as the knowledge penetrated the numbness. Automatically she reached for her handkerchief to dry her face, perhaps to stem the flow a little. Her hand sought in vain for a pocket and brought realisation back to her. Her skirt and sweater were both on the locker, where she had folded them when she had taken them off.

She forced her trembling limbs to carry her across the small cabin, and retrieved the tiny lace-edged linen square from her skirt pocket. She started to wipe her face dry, then froze as voices came towards her door from along the corridor. She gathered her strength together and moved swiftly. She stumbled to the door and with trembling hands ran the fastener into place, shutting herself in. The voices came closer, and then receded. A series of cheerful 'good-nights' were exchanged in several different languages, then silence dropped again. Margaret could hear her own quick breathing, and the thump of her own heart.

'I'm being silly,' she remonstrated herself with a weak laugh, and pulled herself off the door. 'I've allowed Dom to frighten me.' He had intended to, and she had stupidly succumbed to a fear which she told herself was not justified.

Any more than she was justified—the laugh died, and the hot tears returned—any more than she was justified in falling in love with a man who she knew would never allow himself to fall in love with her.

CHAPTER NINE

A LIFETIME passed before it got light. A lifetime during which Margaret relived every one of Dom's kisses, and flayed herself unmercifully with the humiliating reason why he had bestowed them. To teach her a lesson.

'I've learned it by heart,' she assured herself grimly as she rose unrefreshed but dry-eyed the next morning. She had no watch to tell her what time it was, but she could guess well enough to suit her purpose. She blessed I/C Vessel's enthusiastic description of the working of the rig the evening before, and the fact that, in spite of her preoccupation at the time, she had been able to take in enough of what he said to remember the bits that were useful to her.

'The rig crew work twelve hour shifts, rotating at seven a.m. and seven p.m.'

'It must be about that now,' she decided. A stir and bustle of activity from the corridor outside her door aroused her, indicating that one shift might be coming off duty and the other going on. She waited until everything went quiet again before she ventured outside. Dom had told her to wait until daylight. Well, she had waited. Quite long enough.

She came to a decision during the night, and prepared to act upon it now. Crying oneself to sleep was a misnomer, she discovered. She cried, but she did not sleep. And during the long, wakeful hours after Dom left the cabin, her tears crystallised into a burning resentment against him. She hated him for using her so. For cynically arousing her feelings, and then throwing them back in her face, and for the sharp, throbbing pain it left in the empty space where they had lodged. And because he was responsible for the loss of her watch.

She thought hard about her watch. If she thought about it hard enough, it might blot out the thought of Dom. She lay back in the bunk—Dom's bunk—and stared unseeingly into the darkness, living again the moment when the watch bracelet caught the wool of his sweater sleeve, snapped open, and flew in an arc high above their heads and over the side of the rig. But she had not actually *seen* it go over the side of the rig and disappear into the sea, she realised. She screwed up her forehead in an effort of concentration, trying to recall in detail exactly what had happened. She remembered turning away, unable to watch her precious possession go overboard; turning on Dom, and venting her overwrought feelings on him. But *she had not actually seen her watch disappear overboard.*

The realisation hit her like a bolt from the blue, and she sat upright in the bunk, her desire for sleep vanished. Perhaps her watch had not gone into the water after all. Perhaps even now it was caught up somewhere, hanging from part of the superstructure of the rig; swinging in the wind, not sunk beneath the wild green waves. But perhaps in imminent danger of being so, if it was not already. From that moment on she knew no rest until the first streaks of daylight penetrated the gloom. There might still be a chance for her to recover her precious possession. As if to confirm her resolution, a cheerful voice called out from the corridor to someone close by,

'What's it been like up top during the night?'

It must be a member of the new shift, wanting a preview of conditions from his returning opposite number.

'Pretty rough,' another voice responded laconically, 'but it's simmering down now. If it keeps on like this, we should be able to start drilling again before very long.'

I/C Vessel mentioned the evening before, Margaret remembered, that drilling had had to be suspended temporarily because of the severity of the storm. If they were thinking of starting work again, it must mean it was safe to go out on deck. She listened intently. The climatic tantrum above her head still seemed to be in full swing, but—no, the voice had been quite correct. It did not sound quite so violent as before. Probably there was always a certain degree of roughness to be encountered this far out to sea, she reasoned. The rig was unlike a moving ship, it would present a stationary obstacle against which the waves would hurl themselves, even on a calm day. Similar to the sea wall that circled the harbour at Meldonmouth, and against which she never tired of watching the endless rhythm of the beating waters.

She could remember the exact spot on the deck where Dom had caught and held her. Where she had flung her arm to free herself from his hold, and from where her watch had flown. So sure was she of the precise place that it might have been painted in bright colours. Keeping a wary eye open for Dom—it would be just like him to appear when he was least wanted, she thought crossly—she waited until the corridor outside her door was clear, and made her way cautiously towards the upper deck. She reached it undetected, but, her eyes widened with dismay, the surrounding sea did not appear to be simmering down at all. Boiling over might be a better description. Rivers of water streamed from the deck from waves of mountainous height, and instead of standing safely above the surface of the water the rig was dwarfed by waves higher than she had ever seen before.

The wind caught her as she emerged into the open, and she grabbed at the door for support. Just as she had clung to Dom when he helped her out of his car. The thought of the geologist spurred her into action. If he saw her, he would undoubtedly drag her back below decks, if only to show his authority, and her chance to recover her watch would be irretrievably lost.

'He doesn't have any authority over me.' The thought steeled her determination. She would just take one quick look to satisfy herself. If her watch was caught up on anything, it should be easy enough to spot, the platinum would gleam even in the dull light from the stormy morning sky.

'If I go now, I'll miss the next big wave.'

She had watched the waves against the harbour wall often enough, and they seemed to resolve themselves into a more or less regular pattern of small waves, and then a big one every so often. The same probably applied out here. It must have been a particularly big wave—she tried not to think how big—that had put the deck under such a depth of water. It was draining away rapidly now, so now was the time to go.

'If I don't, I'll lose my courage,' she told herself with a fearful glance around her. 'And I'll always wonder, afterwards, and regret not having gone to see.' She pushed the door wide open against the jam. 'I'll leave it open as a bolthole, just in case.' Having an escape route gave her courage the final impetus it needed.

She took a deep breath and forced herself right out on to the open deck. She gasped as the full force of the wind hit her, taking her breath, plucking at her clothes, bringing stinging tears to her eyes, so that momentarily she could not see. She rubbed her hand across them, then grasped hurriedly at a nearby tarpaulin-covered something or other whose shrouded shape defied identification.

She hesitated. This was far worse than she had imagined.

Too late, she realised her own sense of what constituted bad storm conditions came nowhere near the scale used by the rig crew. The wind raised its voice and screamed, 'Danger!' The waves roared an angry threat, and her own unstable stance entreated her to go back while there was still time. And then her eyes caught a dull gleam, high up near the edge of the platform. She could not see what it was, except that it was light striking on metal. It must be her watch.

'I must go and find out.'

She closed her ears to the warning of the wind; defied the slippery deck and her own unsteady feet, and totally miscalculated the rhythm of the waves. Perhaps the storm scorned the habits of the meeker water nearer to the shore, and made every wave a big one.

It headed straight for the rig with a hissing roar, and the speed of an express train. Fear paralysed her limbs, denying her the ability to retreat. She looked up. The wave towered twenty feet over the rig deck, blotting out the light, a huge green darkness, curling like a monster hand reaching out to grab a helpless prey. It was such a wave as Margaret had heard the Meldonmouth fishermen describe as 'all sea', and never realised what they meant until now. Her horrified eyes could detect no white, frothy tip; just a solid weight of water, that any second now would hit the side of the rig and, breaking, descend upon the deck. Upon herself. She screamed as it broke.

'Dom! Dom!'

The sheer weight of it knocked her feet from under her and flattened her on the deck as if she was of no more consequence than a mosquito. It bore down on her with breath-expelling force. Her mind just had time to register the vow, 'I'll go back to the cabin and stay there, the moment the water drains off,' when the receding water picked her up in the undertow and pulled her inexorably towards the side of the rig. Horror lent her a frantic strength, and she flailed wildly, trying to regain her feet. A brief second's purchase on the deck brought her sudden hope, and then her foot slipped, the rubber sole, so suitable for ward rounds, rendered useless on the streaming boards. The suction of the water turned her on her back, helpless as a rag doll against its power, and as if in a slow motion film she caught a glimpse of light gleaming on metal. The gleam she had risked her life to go and look at, and now saw that it was merely a piece of chain link attached to some mechanical equipment lashed to the deck. It was not her watch, after all. The skeletal frame of the derrick swayed above her, passing her. In another second she would be over the side of the rig.

'Dom!'

Water filled her mouth, stifling her scream. The sides of the rig were split seconds away.

'Hold on!'

A strong hand grasped her arm. It slipped, and grasped again, and this time held on. No matter that the hand hurt, with a pressure that felt as if it must split her arm in two. She felt like a rope being used in a tug-of-war between the waves and the hand. Unbelievably, the strength of the hand challenged the strength of the waters—and won.

'Duck, there's another one coming!' The voice that shouted above the wind belonged to Dom. She had cried to him for help, and he had come. His hands guided her frozen fingers to what felt like a steel bar.

'Hold tight! Whatever you do, don't let go. . . .'

The second wave hit them with a solid wall of water and cut off the sound of his voice. It engulfed them, pressing them to the deck, then rushed on, over the side of the rig. Margaret felt the lift and drag of the undertow, trying like a hungry beast to claw them both into its lair. But Dom's arm remained tight around her. He was only holding on himself with one hand, but it was enough. She gripped the steel bar with the strength of desperation, and pressed her face against the wool of his jersey, and in spite of the suffocating pressure of the water that made it feel as if she would never breathe air again, she felt safe, because Dom was with her. At last the endless, sucking pull of the undertow eased, and she fell back limply, gasping for breath.

'Let's go, before another one hits us.'

He did not allow her any respite to get her breath back. With a quick heave he pulled her unceremoniously to her feet, and when she swayed he swung her up high into his arms and ran. From over his shoulder she saw another wave approaching, but because she was in Dom's arms it had lost its threat. She even noted, with a detached sort of calm through a temporary gap in the heaving waters, that the standby vessel had come in a good deal closer to the rig than when she had seen it from the helicopter the day before. It seemed to be approaching them crabwise, but perhaps it was only the angle from which she was looking at it.

'Made it!'

Dom ducked inside the door to below decks, the one she had left open, just as the next wave hit the rig. He turned round and kicked the barrier shut behind him as green water hurled deep across the spot where they had stood seconds before, and then he leaned back against the door, breathing hard, letting her slide out of his arms, and back on to her feet again. She turned to him impulsively and held out her arms, careless that she revealed her feelings. She owed him her life.

'If it hadn't been for you. . . .'

'If it hadn't been for you leaving this door open,' he interrupted her savagely, rejecting her advance, 'I wouldn't even have known you were out on deck.'

'How did you know it was me?' she returned defensively, shaken by his curtness. 'It might have been one of the rig crew.'

'These doors are designed to keep the water out. None of the rig crew would have been so senseless as to leave one open in seas like this. It had to be you,' he told her cuttingly, and added with biting sarcasm, 'If you're bent on collecting a medal for coming out in a gale to succour a beleagured oil rig, for goodness' sake make sure it's not a posthumous one!'

Glory-seeking....

Her face flamed. 'Who said anything about collecting a medal?' she cried furiously. 'I wish I'd never set eyes on the oil rig! I wish your Board of Directors had listened to the other two geologists, instead of to you, and taken your beastly rig miles away. The other geologists were probably right about where the oil is, anyway,' she flung at him angrily, and saw his face tighten, but she was past caring. 'The moment I can go ashore, I'll do so.' How dare he suggest she came out to the rig seeking medals?

'The quicker you're back on shore the better,' he retorted bluntly. 'We've got enough problems to sort out here as it is, without adding you to our responsibilities as well.'

Margaret had not thought of herself as a responsibility. A sole woman among eighty men, on an oil rig in the middle of a gale, would come under that category, she realised guiltily, and then her chin came up proudly. However Dom regarded her, she came out to the rig as a doctor, not as a woman—a responsibility. An encumbrance?

'Problems like trying to convince people there's oil to be found where there isn't?' she thrust back at him swiftly.

'The oil underneath where we stand is as certain as the sea surrounding us,' he brushed aside her jibe contemptuously. 'Of all the crazy things to do,' he burst out, 'to go out on deck with seas running this high. Have you taken leave of your senses?'

'How was I to know they'd crash over the rig deck like that?'

'You must have felt the force of them build up during the night.'

She had. The shuddering crashes accompanied her dreams like a continuous drum roll until daylight. But she had never in her wildest nightmares visualised anything so bad as this.

'I didn't know,' she began weakly.

'I/C Vessel warned you about the risk of being washed overboard. I heard him myself.'

'I thought he was joking.'

'Joking?' He stared at her incredulously. 'Do you think it's a joke, to risk being sucked into a sea like that? What chance do you think you'd have had out there?' he stormed at her angrily. 'The quicker we can get the Chinook airborne and you in it heading for shore, the better for everyone's peace of mind,' he finished unflatteringly.

'I won't need to wait for the helicopter,' she retorted spiritedly, 'I'll go ashore with the standby vessel. It's coming towards the rig, so it's probably going to head for harbour afterwards.' What chance she would have of transferring from the rig to the vessel in such a storm she did not pause to consider.

'The standby vessel's anchored a good way off from us,' Dom dismissed her comment as irrelevant.

'It's no such thing, it's close by, and coming in fast. I saw it myself.' Did he think she was suffering from hallucinations? she asked herself indignantly. 'It was approaching us sideways.' She underlined her observation with triumphant exactitude, and had the satisfaction of seeing him pause. He glanced at her with suddenly keen attention.

'Sideways? Are you sure?'

'Of course I'm sure, I know which is the side of a ship, and which is the back and front.'

His lips twitched momentarily, and she opened her mouth to rectify her blunder, to show him she knew which was fore and aft. She might be land-based, but she was not totally ignorant of seafaring matters.

'Sparks!' Dom shouted urgently at a figure hurrying past at the end of the corridor, denying her chance to speak. The figure paused, and turned.

'Can't stop now, Mr Orr, I'm....'

'You'll have to stop for this.' Dom hurried to join him, dragging Margaret along in his wake. 'Doctor Warrender here says the standby vessel is drifting sideways in towards the rig.' He did not say how she had come to learn what she spoke of, indeed his tone still questioned her statement, she thought angrily.

'I saw it. . . .'

'Doc's right, sir, it is,' the radio operator spoke hurriedly. 'The vessel radioed us to say they've got engine failure, and their anchor's dragging. They're working like fiends to get her under way again, but unless they're quick, they'll ram us for sure.'

'On your way to I/C Vessel, and get the alarm sounded.' Dom waved the man off on his errand, and took hold of Margaret by the arm. 'Come with me.' He pulled her with him towards the sick bay door and hastened inside. Her patient lay easily in his bunk, deep in the inevitable magazine on hang-gliding.

'Get up quick, the alarm's going to sound.' Dom removed his magazine and pulled back the covers without ceremony, then turned to Margaret. 'I shall be about two minutes. Help the M.O. until I come back.' He vanished through the door just as an unearthly wail sounded through the rig.

'What's up?' The M.O. did not need any second bidding, he was already halfway out of the bunk, and reaching for his clothes.

'The standby vessel's got engine failure, and her anchor's dragging.' Margaret wasted no time, she helped him slide his plastered leg into his trousers. 'The radio operator seemed afraid they'd ram us.'

'If they're that close in, he's got good cause,' her patient rejoined briefly. 'Where's Dom gone to?'

'I'm back.' The geologist came through the door and tossed an odd-looking arrangement of materials and straps in the direction of the M.O. 'Get this on, quickly. I'll help Margaret.' He shook out a second similar piece of equipment in his hand and turned her round in front of him. 'Stand still.' With practised fingers he strapped her into the lifebelt. 'Stay with the M.O. and do whatever he tells you,' he instructed her tersely. 'I'm going up to see what's happening. I'll be back.'

'Where's your lifebelt?' He had only got the two in his hand when he came through the door.

'I'll go back and collect one,' he began evasively, and fear rose sharp inside her.

'You've given me yours.' He was without one, and if the ship rammed the rig.... Her fingers tore at the straps he had fastened round her, frantic to undo them.

'Leave them alone.' He gripped her hands, preventing her from carrying out her intention.

'You haven't got a lifebelt.'

'I can swim.' Incredibly, his teeth flashed white in a grin.

'What chance do you think you'd have, out there?' she sobbed on a rising note of desperation, using his own words against him. 'Dom, you must....'

As long as she lived, Margaret never forgot the dull, grinding crump! as the standby vessel hit the side of the rig.

The world gave a sickening lurch. The deck tilted at a crazy angle beneath her feet, righted itself, and tilted again. Men shouted. Doors banged, and the other end of the sick bay rushed towards her at speed. She put up her arms to shelter her face, saw a high cupboard door snap open and swing wildly, and a pile of something white disgorge itself from the interior. The assorted mixture of pillows and blankets broke her landing against the bottom of the cupboard. She hit it sideways on, completely out of control—like the standby vessel, the thought flashed across her mind—then she was buried in a welter of soft whiteness, and something solid and heavy landed on top. Panic-stricken, she tried to struggle free, and the weight lifted itself off her.

'Sorry, I couldn't stop myself.' Dom searched among the bedding and lifted her free. 'Are you hurt?'

'No, just squashed.' She raised her eyes to his face, and went white. 'You're bleeding!'

'It's nothing much,' he dabbed at the red stream oozing

from a cut across his forehead. 'I'm taller than you are. I hit the cupboard door,' he said ruefully.

'I'll sue you, if you've damaged my surgery furniture.' The M.O. slid across the floor on his back, and joined them in an undignified rush.

'For goodness' sake mind your leg,' Margaret cried, then she started to laugh, weakly.

'I don't see what's funny,' her patient complained.

'Neither do I.' Dom eyed her narrowly, plainly suspecting hysteria.

'It's your M.O. I told him hang-gliding was dangerous,' Margaret burbled, unable to help herself. 'It's nothing compared to an oil rig!'

An answering glint lit Dom's eyes, and his teeth flashed in a grin.

'So it is dangerous,' he agreed, 'people can get broken legs following hobbies like that. . . .'

'You two might at least help me up!'

The geologist's eyes met Margaret's above the head of her indignantly protesting patient as together they helped him to his feet, and she caught her breath sharply. For the first time since they met, Dom's vivid blue eyes held neither censure nor anger, nor even a challenge. Just the light of pure laughter, and it set her heart singing in a way that made light of the gale, and the collision, and the danger. Because the laughter forged a link between them, fragile, intangible, and born of the emergency, but precious because it was shared.

CHAPTER TEN

THE brief, intimate moment was gone.

'Get ready for action.' The M.O. took charge. Injured he might be, but he drew his own conclusions from the noises filtering down from above, and prepared to cope with the consequences. 'Find out what's happening aloft, and let us know, will you Dom?'

The blue eyes left Margaret's and turned to the M.O., the laughter gone, and she felt as if a light had been switched off, leaving her in darkness. But there was no time to think about her own feelings now. A figure appeared at the door, supporting another. The one doing the supporting was the roustabout of her earlier acquaintance, his face still criss-crossed with the stitches she had inserted.

'You again!' she exclaimed involuntarily.

'Not me this time, lady,' he grinned. In spite of the awfulness of their predicament, he still grinned. Margaret felt an immense respect amounting almost to awe rise within her towards these oil men. 'It's the tool pusher here. I guess he's got some ribs stove in.' He might have been saying, 'he's got a good book to read.' Their casualness was amazing.

'Put him down here,' The M.O. instructed, then when the roustabout's hands were free, 'now steady me, will you? I'm not making a very good job of standing on one leg.' He worked on the one side of the stretcher, and Margaret worked from the other. Dom left them to go aloft. Margaret did not actually see him go, but she sensed when he was no longer there. There was an emptiness, a feeling that she was suddenly, dreadfully alone, no matter that the M.O. and the roustabout were there, and the injured man between them. She worked on, closing her mind to everything but the task in hand. And then the emptiness vanished. Even before Dom spoke she knew he had come back, although she was turned away from the door she could feel his presence reach her across the room.

'Here's another one for you, and there's two more to bring down yet.'

A dislocated shoulder, broken fingers, and a case of concussion followed in quick succession, until the tiny sick bay began to resemble a battlefield. The brunt of the work of necessity fell to Margaret. The M.O. laboured valiantly, but he was handicapped by his plastered leg, and even with the roustabout's assistance it was all he could do to maintain his equilibrium on the wildly unstable deck. Margaret began to fear that tiredness and instability might make him her next casualty.

Dom seemed to be everywhere at once. He ferried in the injured men, fetched and carried about the sick bay, and lent a hand with the patients, doing what was necessary without once having to be asked. And all the time a hideous grinding, rubbing sound, that Margaret sensed correctly was the standby vessel being ground against the side of the rig by the pounding waves, kept up a terrifying background accompaniment to her work. How long could any vessel take such a battering before it fell apart? she wondered desperately. And if it did.... She felt she would scream if the noise did not soon cease.

Unexpectedly, it did. A heaving lurch sent them grabbing for support at the nearest thing handy. It was followed almost instantly by a juddering crash, which felt as if it would split the rig in two. Another lurch, and Dom exclaimed,

'They've got her under way. Thank God!'

She felt, rather than heard, the vessel's engines start. A low mechanical throb vibrated through the rig; coughed, halted. A tense silence held the occupants of the sick bay for what seemed a thousand years. Margaret's eyes flew to Dom's face, but he did not turn to look at her. His head was raised, listening, his face taut.

'She's free.'

He relaxed as the throb strengthened and grew firm and regular, and the sound of a ragged cheer filtered through the bulkheads. The deck under their feet resumed its normal level with disconcerting suddenness as the vessel pulled itself clear of the rig, and the M.O. grabbed Margaret and held on tightly to her as she staggered out of control against him. Relieved laughter rippled round the sick bay, the tension released like the snapping of taut elastic.

'You won't need me any more, doc,' the roustabout discovered he had other things to do.

'No, but thanks for your help, just the same.' The M.O. released him, but he did not release Margaret. 'And thank you for yours, too,' he said teasingly—and kissed her full on the lips. 'You've been absolutely fabulous!' he exclaimed admiringly.

She felt herself go scarlet. If Dom had not been there, she would not have minded. She would have taken his kiss in the spirit it was intended, and probably returned it, out of sheer relief from tension. But Dom was there. He stood right beside her, looking on. She raised her chin, refusing to feel embarrassed. At least her colleague approved of her being on the rig, she thought proudly. To the M.O. she was not an encumbrance. She was fabulous! And she did not in the least mind him saying so. She was glad he had done so in front of Dom, she thought defiantly.

'I quite agree,' Dom drawled. She turned, startled, not expecting him to agree, and the M.O. released her into his arms. He lifted her effortlessly clear of the floor, just as he had done in her cottage after the party.

'Thanks for your help—Margaret.'

Laughter lurked in his eyes, and he repeated the M.O.'s salutation casually, teasingly. The patients in the sick bay looked on with interested eyes, and Margaret went hot with mortification.

'Put me down at once!' she hissed furiously. She could take a kiss as a joke from the M.O., but not from Dom. What the feel of Dom's lips did to her when they touched her own, even lightly, as now, was not a joke.

He put her down, gently, his face laughing into hers, enjoying her confusion. She felt an urge to slap him, but the patients were looking on, and so was the M.O., so she swallowed hard and took a grip on herself, and somehow managed a shaky laugh. She congratulated herself on the laugh. It sounded almost natural. No one would suspect how she felt. She looked up and met two blue, dancing eyes, and knew she had no cause for congratulation so far as Dom was concerned. He did not suspect. He knew!

'I'll clear up in here while I can, before anything else happens.' Somehow she got the words out almost normally, although it took all her willpower to turn away from Dom, away from his arms. She felt bereft when he let her go, and her unsteadiness could not entirely be blamed on the storm-beleaguered rig.

'Nothing else is likely to happen now, the storm's blowing itself out.' I/C Vessel came through the door to check on how they had fared.

'In that case, it shouldn't be too long before the helicopter can take off.' Margaret did not try to hide the relief in her voice. 'You take a rest now,' she told the M.O. crisply. 'I'll prepare the patients for transfer to the shore hospital.' How good it felt to be back inside her armour once more! She would be transferring with the injured men. Away from the rig, and Dom's world—away from Dom. Once she was safely back in her own domain again she could take stock of herself and regain some sort of control over her emotions, that had run riot in unison with the weather since she came to the oil rig. She needed time to stand outside herself, and consider, and she could not do that while Dom was near her. If he remained on the rig, there would be no chance of them meeting, even accidentally.

'Let me know when the pilot can take off,' Dom spoke to I/C Vessel. 'I'll go ashore at the same time.'

'But....' Margaret turned, nonplussed, a half folded sheet stilled in her hands.

'There'll be plenty of room in the Chinook.' The geologist slanted her an oblique glance. 'I'm on leave—remember?'

She had forgotten. If he came ashore there was a chance he might visit the hospital to see the men from the rig. Perhaps bump into her accidentally on the wards.... She made up her mind swiftly.

'Will you contact the hospital by radio-telephone, and

ask them to have an ambulance waiting at the airport?' she asked I/C Vessel, and added, as if casually, 'Tell them I'll remain on the rig until you get a replacement M.O.'

She did not look at Dom as she said it. She dared not, for fear of the anger she knew she would find in his face. And she did not pause to consider what difficulties her decision might cause on the rig. She only knew she must remain outside Dom's orbit at all costs.

'You'll do nothing of the kind.'

She did not need to look at him to see that she had made him angry. It vibrated in his voice reaching out to her in a solid, implacable wall of opposition. Her eyes flashed green fire, and she raised them defiantly to look at him.

'I'll do whatever. . . .'

'It's most kind of you, Doctor Warrender, but it won't be necessary,' I/C Vessel interrupted in his mild manner. 'There'll be a doctor waiting at the air-strip to come back with the helicopter. We've recalled our other man from leave until the M.O. here is back in action again.'

There was no help for it. She had to go. Once again the geologist had prevailed. It was no satisfaction to her that his victory this time was a coincidence over which he had no more control than she herself.

'While you're still here, Doc, will you unstitch me?' The roustabout reappeared at the door, cheerfully oblivious of the tense undercurrents he interrupted, and Margaret turned to him thankfully.

'It's too early to take your stitches out,' she began, then she looked at his face and saw that it was not. Clean salty air had completed the process of healing in half the usual time, and his cuts no longer needed the aid of stitches. 'All right, come along in,' she agreed, 'I'll take them out for you now. Pull a chair up—here.' Deliberately, she indicated the spot on which Dom stood, and had the satisfaction of seeing him scowl. He should not have his own way in everything, she determined mutinously, and while she was working in the sick bay she would remain in charge, for however short a period it might be.

'Doc, while you're here, can you spare me a minute? I've collected a splinter....'

Out of nowhere a line of patients appeared at the door. They all looked remarkably healthy to Margaret, and she regarded them with some puzzlement. There appeared to be an epidemic of splinters. One man complained of having something in his eye, but it did not seem to affect his interested appraisal of herself.

'I was never this popular,' the M.O. joked, with more than a grain of truth, and a quirk of laughter bubbled inside Margaret as the reason for the line dawned on her. The rig crew were curious about the new woman M.O., and those who had not seen her were coming down to have a look for themselves, using any excuse that presented itself. She raised amused eyes and met Dom's angry glare.

'If I'm in the way....' he began savagely, and she smiled up at him.

'You are,' she told him sweetly.

He glowered at her, blackly. If I didn't know better, I should think he was jealous, she thought, and then her amusement died as he turned on his heel without a word, and quit the room, and she could have wept because he was not jealous, and she wished with all her heart he might be. She removed the stitches from the roustabout's face, and despatched the rest of the men without loss of time, and the M.O. grinned.

'They're not going to like my stand-in after this.'

'We're not off the rig yet,' she retorted shortly. Wearily, she longed to be ashore. She felt battered, by the gale, and by her own feelings, and she yearned for the peace and solitude of her own cottage. Something of her feelings must have shown on her face, because the M.O. looked across at her sympathetically.

'It shouldn't be too long now, the gale's dying out rapidly.'

By midday it had subsided to a strong wind. Nervously

Margaret emerged on the deck, and could hardly believe the difference that met her eyes. The mountainous waves of a few short hours before were gone as if they had never been. There was still a heavy swell running, alarming enough in ordinary circumstances, but her early morning experience had armoured her against it. Even the stiff wind that tossed her curls into a fiery halo round her head seemed by comparison to be no more than a slight breeze.

'Have your lunch before you set off. We owe you that, at least.'

She sat down to another superb meal, for which she had no appetite, because once again Dom sat at the opposite side of the table from her. Resolutely she kept her eyes on her plate, refusing to look up in case she met his eyes. Most of the rig men ate in silence, she noticed, so her own behaviour looked in no way peculiar. Their eating habits mirrored those she was accustomed to at the hospital. For people with a purpose, daytime meals could not be relaxing social occasions, they ate because they were hungry, and spent as little time about it as possible before recommencing work.

'We're ready to take off as soon as we're loaded, Doc.' The pilot finished his meal and rose from the table, and Margaret did the same, released from the torment of having to pretend to eat.

'I'll get the patients up on deck.'

'I'll come and give you a hand.' Dom rose, too.

She could not get rid of him. Why didn't he stay and finish his coffee, and leave her to do her job in peace?

'I can manage.' She meant it to sound crushing, but she might as well not have spoken.

'The patients may need help to stand, it's still blowing hard, and I don't want my colleagues damaged any more than they are at present,' he retorted drily, eyeing her lack of inches with unflattering calculation.

'I'll help Dom,' the pilot cut across her furious rejoinder. 'He's right, the old ship's still a bit unsteady, and they may need a stout arm on either side,' he said tactfully, ignoring

Margaret's own efforts to remain steady on her feet.

'Thank you.' She gave way as gracefully as she could. She did not thank Dom. She did not want his help, though when the two men ferried her patients to the helicopter one at a time and settled them in their seats, she realised she could not have managed the job on her own. She was not tall enough to be of sufficient support, nor steady enough on the constantly moving deck.

She looked about her at the rash of activity that had broken out since the storm subsided. Men worked on the side of the rig repairing the damage caused by the stand-by vessel, which had now, she noticed, resumed its station at a safe distance from the rig. She could see antlike figures swarming at its side, presumably engaged in the same kind of repair work.

'Your turn now.'

She was so engrossed in watching the activity on deck, she had not noticed all her patients were safely installed in the big Chinook. Dom came up behind her, and before she could utter more than a gasp of protest he picked her up easily and swung her high in his arms.

'Put me down!' she demanded furiously. 'I'm quite capable of getting in without your help.'

'I'm merely making sure you don't get left behind,' he retorted grimly, and swung her into a seat in front of the M.O.

'There's no need to hem me in, either,' she protested angrily as he lowered her into the window seat and deliberately sat down beside her so that she could not get out unless he let her through.

'I'm merely making sure,' he reiterated unflatteringly, with a grin that brought a hot tide of furious colour to her face.

'Here we go, folks. Meldonmouth next stop!'

The pilot did something to the controls, the rotor spun into life above them, and imperceptibly at first and then more rapidly the rig fell away from them. Margaret turned abruptly away from Dom, presenting her shoulder to him, and returned I/C Vessel's farewell wave with more fervour than she might otherwise have shown.

'Gee, that was some storm last night. Just look down there!'

An endless strain of silence later, the pilot's awestruck exclamation drew their attention downwards, and Margaret went weak with relief as she discovered the rapidly approaching coastline below them. Thank goodness! Another ten minutes or so and she would be in the ambulance on her way back to the hospital along with her patients, and Dom, and the oil rig, and the whole unwelcome episode would be behind her.

'Those fishing smacks sure caught a pounding.'

Her eyes widened with dismay as they followed the pilot's gesture.

'Those two look as if they're well beached.' Dom leaned over her to look out of the window, his shoulder hard against her own, pressing her, and she stiffened resentfully, but willy-nilly her attention was drawn downwards to the shingle as they passed over it.

'There's another.' A third fishing smack lay on its side, slewed high on the beach, far above the normal waterline, like a stranded whale left by the receding tide.

'I wonder if I've got any slates left on my cottage.' Visions of the greengrocer's denuded roof sent Margaret's eyes seeking anxiously along the doll houses below them.

'We're coming in from the other side of the harbour. We're too far away to be able to pick out any detail on your cottage.'

He was right, of course. He always was. She shrugged, and turned away from the window, feigning disinterest, unwilling to admit that she was completely disorientated. It took her some time to recognise their exact whereabouts from the unfamiliar viewpoint of the chimneypots, and by the time she was able to pick out which part of the harbour her own cottage lay, they were already turning away, dropping down towards the air-strip on the outer perimeter of the town.

Less than ten minutes now.

She peered downwards again, and caught sight of the ambulance already drawn up beside the huddle of huts that served as a waiting room, store, and general offices. Her heart began to pound. The oblong, bleak-looking vehicle represented escape. Once she and her patients were inside, and the big double doors were shut behind them, Dom could do as he pleased, she thought hardly. She would not offer him a lift into town. He travelled to and from the rig often enough to have some means of transport available, even if his own car was not there. She did not care if he had to walk back....

'Stay here, while I go and see the ambulance driver.' He got up from beside her as the helicopter settled to rest.

'I won't stay here!' Margaret breathed angrily. His instruction might be heeded by her patients, but she certainly did not intend to obey it. She jumped to her feet mutinously. Dom had left his world behind him on the rig. This was her domain now, and if there were any instructions to be given she would give them. She opened her mouth to tell him so, and then saw that neither Dom's intervention nor her own was necessary. The ambulance backed up to the helicopter, efficiently guided by a tall, black-haired figure in a white coat.

'Bill!'

'Hi, Maggie,' the house surgeon waved cheerily. 'How was the ship's biscuit?'

He lifted her down and set her on her feet in front of him, his shrewd glance reading the dark shadows under her eyes. She did not mind Bill holding her. She did not mind Bill quizzing her. If it had not been for the fact that they were in full view of the others, she would have flung her arms round his neck and kissed him.

Dear Bill! Dear, familiar Bill, from her own familiar world, where storms meant slates being blown off roofs, and having to repair the consequences in dented heads, and storms of emotion—at least so far as she was concerned—simply did not exist.

'The ship's biscuit was fine.' She would tell him all about it later. Perhaps not quite all, she compromised cautiously. 'How was the hospital?'

'Running quite smoothly without you,' he grinned teasingly. 'Neil came back yesterday with another medic, which is why I'm here now. The Chief says you're to go straight home and have a good rest, and get over your adventure before you report back to the General,' he instructed firmly.

She did not resent Bill telling her what to do, but she wished he had not couched the instruction in quite those terms. That was how Dom thought she regarded the whole episode—as an adventure.

'You're off duty as of now.' Bill mimicked her own words to him of several nights ago. He turned her hand round, pushed up her sleeve to check the time, and paused.

'What's happened to your watch? I've never known you to be without it before. Has the bracelet fastening gone altogether?' he asked innocently.

'Yes—overboard,' Margaret answered curtly. She did not look at Dom.

'You mean you lost it, from the rig? Oh, Maggie, I *am* sorry!' Bill's face creased with concern. 'If only....'

'It can't be undone, so it's no use mourning.' She stopped Bill before he could go any further. She had given Dom no explanation as to why she, and not Bill, had answered the call from the rig, and she did not intend to do so now.

'That's the lot, Doctor Quinn. We're ready to go.' The orderly finished transferring the patients from the helicopter to the ambulance, and approached Bill. He looked a question at Margaret.

'I'll beg a lift back with you, and then go straight home.' She felt grateful for Neil's consideration. She was even more tired than she had realised.

'You'll have to sit on my lap,' Bill warned her cheerfully. 'The old battlewagon's full with four patients inside. Neil's come back with the promise of a new ambulance for us, as well,' he informed her in a satisfied tone.

'I'll give Margaret a lift home. My car's parked in the hanger.'

She wished Neil had brought the new ambulance back with him. Anything would be preferable to riding in the two-seater with Dom.

'I'll go with....' She was going to say, 'I'll go with you in the ambulance.'

'Fine, then we'll be off. See you on Sunday, Maggie—that is, if the party's still on?'

'Yes—yes, of course.'

The house surgeon completely misunderstood her. Before she could call him back the ambulance started to roll, and he was out of earshot—out of reach. And unless she accepted Dom's offer of a lift it would be she who would have to walk back.

'Stay there, I'll go and fetch the car.'

This time she did stay. There seemed nothing else for her to do. Of a sudden, a wave of depression hit her. Since she had met Dom she seemed to have no control over her own life any more. He had prised her out of her armour like a winkle on the end of a pin, she thought disgustedly. Only the pin had turned into a sword that pierced her to the very heart. Life had completely changed. She had changed, even before she went to the rig. And then she had spent two days on the rig, and life would never be the same again.

'Give me your case, I'll put it in the back.'

She gave him her case, watched him put it in the back of his car.

'Get in.'

She got in. Without warning, exhaustion poleaxed her. She did as she was told like an automaton. Dom reached across her and slammed the passenger door shut. Then he turned to her, and his voice was hard and cold.

'Are you going to do as your Chief says, or are you going your own stubborn way, as usual, and returning to the hospital?'

'Do I have any choice, with you driving?' Her voice was high, and sharp, her capacity to battle back rapidly evaporating.

'Not unless you want to walk back from your cottage.' He watched her for a long moment, which seemed like a lifetime before he spoke again. 'It's a pity your Chief wasn't here when the call was received from the rig. You wouldn't be in this state now....'

'It was my decision to come out. It had nothing to do with you. You make the decisions in your job, I make them in mine. Surely even you can see that?'

Margaret felt beyond caring whether he saw it or not. Her voice was flat with tiredness. Her emotions were temporarily lulled, anaesthetised under a solid layer of exhaustion. She leaned back in her seat and closed her eyes. If he did not start the engine soon she would go to sleep in the car, and then he would have another problem—what to do with her. She felt too miserable to care what he did with her.

A solitary tear forced its way below her lashes and rested in the dark hollows underneath her eyes. Her hands stayed motionless in her lap, too weary to lift themselves to wipe it away. Dom sat very still beside her. She could hear his breathing, soft, very faint, but it meant his head must be turned towards her that she could hear it at all. And then he moved. She felt him move, the seats were so close together that the movement transmitted itself to her, even through her closed lids, as he reached out and flicked the ignition, and the engine purred obediently into life. He spoke, and his voice was suddenly not cold and hard any more, but quiet, and oddly gentle.

'I can see it's time I took you home,' he said.

CHAPTER ELEVEN

'WHAT a mess!'

Margaret felt the car stop, felt Dom heave himself out of his seat, and the car rock as the door slammed behind him. His feet crunched on shingle. What was he doing, walking on shingle? He was supposed to be taking her home. With an immense effort of will she prised her eyes open. They gazed blankly through the windscreen at a high wall of shingle, higher than the hood of the car. Without leaning forward to peer through the windshield, she could not see the top of it.

'What have we stopped on the beach for?'

What crazy notion had Dom got into his head now? she wondered. Perhaps he intended her to walk home after all, to teach her a lesson. Just the same as he had kissed her when she was on the rig—to teach her a lesson. Exasperation, and the brief rest during the journey from the air-strip, gave her the strength to get out of the car.

She pushed at the door beside her. It stuck, or perhaps she had not pulled the unfamiliar latch far enough back to clear it. In an upsurge of irritation she put her shoulder against it and pushed, and it sprang open suddenly.

'Careful!' He caught her as she pitched forward, unable to save herself. He lifted her the rest of the way out of the car and set her on her feet beside him.

'What have you parked on the beach for?' she began angrily. And then she saw the roof above the pile of shingle, and the chimneypots above that. Her own roof. And her own chimneypots. Automatically her eyes registered the fact that all the slates were intact. One of the ridge tiles was askew, and a chimneypot on the kitchen side of the cottage leaned at a precarious angle.

127

'We're not on the beach. We're parked as near as I can get to your front door,' he told her grimly. 'Though whether we can reach it through this lot remains to be seen. The storm last night seems to have pushed half the beach up against the cottages.'

Margaret had heard of such things happening, from a grizzled veteran of the fishing fleet who had made a habit of dropping in to see her now and then, but though she enjoyed listening to his tales she had always put down that particular story to a vivid imagination, and an excusable desire on the part of the old man to impress her. The verification of his stories barred her way into her own home at this very moment, hiding it almost to the eaves. She swallowed convusively.

'I'll manage to get in somehow.' She had not the slightest idea how she would manage. The pile of pebbles seemed to grow larger as she looked at it, looming palely in the early dusk. She could climb over it to reach her front door, but she knew from walking on the beach how difficult that would prove. The shingle would roll beneath her feet, sliding her back one step for every two she took upwards. It needed speed to get across such a pile. Only speed, and a good burst of energy, would surmount the ton or so of shingle that the storm had delivered free of charge on her front doorstep, and she did not possess the energy.

'It's too late to start shovelling it away now,' she began doubtfully. She had not got the strength for that, either. She swayed slightly, and Dom's hand found her elbow, steadying her.

'Where's your door key?' he asked.

'In my coat pocket. Why?' To use a door key, you first had to reach the door.

'This pocket?' He did not ask permission. He reached lean brown fingers into the deep slit pockets of her tweed and fished around. He could not miss the key this time, there was nothing else in her pocket except her handkerchief, and his fingers emerged with his quarry firmly gripped between them.

'It's high time you were tucked in bed.'

He stooped and swung her into his arms, and without a pause sprinted straight at the pile of shingle. Incredibly, even burdened with her weight, he maintained sufficient speed to stop himself from slipping backwards as he mounted the sloping side of the pile. With a sinister whispering sound the smooth stones cascaded in miniature landfalls from where his feet dug into them, but by the time they began to move he was already above them, displacing more. He did not start to slide until he was over the top, and facing the equally steep downward slope.

Margaret shut her eyes, and turned her face into his sweater, convinced he must lose his footing; convinced that if he did the pile would slide, and they would both be irretrievably buried.

He slid, but by a superb feat of balancing skill that would have done credit to a tightrope walker in a circus, he kept himself upright. The rolling pebbles, aided by their combined weight, deposited them at speed at the bottom of the heap, almost on to her front doorstep. They skidded to a halt, and he laughed—actually laughed.

'Your windows all seem to be intact.'

Margaret opened her eyes cautiously, and looked up.

'Do you feel strong enough to stand?'

She nodded, bereft for the moment of speech, and he set her on her feet, keeping his arm about her, testing her ability to remain upright on her own.

'The pebbles haven't come right up against the walls of the cottages, either.' He was irritatingly determined to be cheerful. 'The curve of the harbour wall seems to have stopped a lot of them, and the steepness of the slope must have checked them from rolling right in.'

For the first time since she bought the cottage, she blessed the sharp rise up to her front door. If the slope had been in the opposite direction. . . .

'They'll have to be cleared.' Her voice was flat. Even the effort of thinking about clearing away the pile seemed too much in her present frame of mind.

'We'll worry about that tomorrow. It's getting too dark to start on anything like that now.'

It was not his worry, it was hers, but she felt too tired to point it out to him. With a shrug she let it go.

'Your electricity's working, too.' Dom opened the front door with her key and snapped on the light, then propelled her through the miniature hall into the kitchen beyond. Automatically, once she was inside Margaret headed towards the fridge.

'What are you going to do?' The hint of impatience in his voice should have warned her.

'I'm going to make you a cup of coffee—us a cup of coffee.' She was becoming incoherent. Her words sounded slurred. She passed a hand across her eyes. Even through her daze, the obligations of hospitality stirred. Dom had driven her home, she owed him a cup of coffee. Vaguely she recalled offering him a cup of coffee in her kitchen before, and he had refused, she could not remember why.

'You're not going to do anything of the sort.' She recalled him saying something similar to that before as well. A spark of rebellion cleared some of the daze as he took her hand away from the handle of the fridge door with authoritative fingers.

'I'm....' She started to put it back. It was her hand, and her fridge. Her house, in fact.

'You're going to bed.' He turned her round towards him and kissed her, very calmly and very deliberately, full on her lips. It was not the sort of kiss she had come to expect from Dom, it was more as if he was kissing a tired and rather fractious child, and she pulled away from him, resentment flaring in her.

'Or do I have to come and put you there?' he asked silkily, and there was steel in his voice to match the glint in his eyes. She observed it, and paused.

'I'll bring you a hot drink in exactly ten minutes' time.'
He turned towards the fridge and opened it with a purposeful air.

His tone said, 'Be in bed by that time, or else. . . .' Margaret decided not to put it to the test. For one thing, she had not got the strength to battle any more tonight. For another, she had an uneasy conviction she would lose. If she was not tucked up in bed within the stipulated ten minutes, she did not doubt Dom was more than capable of carrying out his threat and putting her there. He sorted out a bottle of milk and a saucepan, poured the contents of the one into the other, and lit the stove. He did not turn round. His back said, 'Ten minutes, and no more.' She stumbled out of the room and pulled herself up the stairs. Two minutes of the ten must already have gone.

Her bedroom was cold. She had left the transom window open when she went out the previous day, never suspecting what adventures would befall her before she reached home again. She shivered. It may not have been entirely due to the temperature of the room that she shivered. Sounds from downstairs indicated that beakers and spoons were being added to the utensils on the stove. She shut the transom window with an unnecessarily loud bang to blot out the sounds.

'It's a good job it's facing away from the direction of the wind.'

If it had not been, she would not have left it open in the first place, but it helped to hear the sound of her own voice talking domestic trivialities. It brought back a sense of proportion—but not her courage. She pulled open a drawer and rummaged it into chaos until she found a pair of pyjamas which she had bought when she was a student, to accompany her on a midwinter walking tour that involved spending several nights under canvas. The blue material was thick and warm, and had a high knitted rib collar and matching cuffs to the long sleeves. Her cheeks warmed as she remembered Dom's reaction on finding her in his cabin clothed in little else but her lacy slip. She did not intend him to see her in an even more revealing nylon nightdress.

The stairs creaked—the middle one always did. Which meant that in about two seconds he would be in the room with her. With a desperate arm she swept her discarded undies out of sight under the eiderdown and dived under the covers herself.

'Brr!' She drew up her knees hurriedly under her chin. The bed was as cold as the room. People who summarily ordered other people to bed, she thought resentfully, should first give a thought to the length of time it takes an electric blanket to make that bed habitable. The shock of the cold widened her eyes into temporary alertness. They widened further still—with apprehension—as footsteps halted outside her door. The footsteps paused, then he knocked. It was not a perfunctory 'bang and then come straight in' sort of knock, more of an 'audible warning' sort, albeit a determined one. And then, to her surprise, he waited.

'C-come in,' she stammered. It must be the cold, making her teeth chatter, she told herself. But it was not the cold that drew her eyes to his in a look that held a depth of mute appeal.

The door swung open at her summons and he ducked his head to come inside. The lintel was of normal height, but Dom made it seem as if it was built to give entry to a dwarf. He stood there looking down at her for a minute of silent regard that seemed like a year. His blue eyes noted her sturdy, high-necked pyjamas, and his lips twitched, and she lowered her eyes, suddenly shy. They alighted on the tray he held in his hands. It contained two beakers. Her interested nose caught the smell of hot chocolate and hot buttered toast, and she realised with surprise that she was hungry as well as tired and cold. Under his arm Dom bore two soft somethings in homely red woollen jackets.

'Hot water bottles? Oh, bless you!' Relief and gratitude overcame her shyness.

'One for your feet.' He put the tray and the one hot water bottle carefully on her bedside table, and deftly separated the top covers from the bottom sheet with his free hand. 'Stretch your feet down, to see if that's about right.' He pushed the first bottle into place.

'It's perfect.' She relaxed with a sigh of bliss as her frozen toes encountered warm, woollen softness.

'And one to cuddle.' He handed her the other, and she glanced up at him, surprised. How did he know...?

'My mother always gave us two, when we were small,' he explained gravely, but there was a twinkle somewhere in the depths of his blue eyes. 'And when you're exhausted, and cold, and frightened, you don't feel very grown-up....'

Margaret was not frightened. She took in an indignant breath to tell him so, then let it out again and remained silent, because she was frightened—just a little—of him.

'Eat your toast and drink your chocolate while they're hot.'

The toast was crunchy, and oozing with butter, and the chocolate was steaming hot, so that she had to sip it slowly, while the blessed warmth of it seeped through her frozen body.

Dom sat on the edge of the bed and drank his with her, in companionable silence. He pushed the eiderdown aside to make room to sit down. She saw his lips curve upwards, and went warmer still as he tactfully tucked an intimate morsel of embroidery and lace back under the seclusion of the eiderdown, then without comment he cupped his hands round his own beaker and sipped too, as if it was the most natural thing in the world that he should be sitting on the side of her bed on a bitter February night, enjoying hot chocolate together.

'Would you like something more to eat?'

She shook her head. Her eyes were closing. She was warm all over, and the room, and Dom, were fast becoming a blur. She slid deep into the pillows and felt him pull the covers close round her, tucking her in, but her lids were too heavy to lift. From a long distance away she heard the beakers being clinked together on the tray, heard the whisper of the door opening and closing across the carpet, and the middle stair creaked under Dom's descending tread. She was slipping over the edge of sleep when she remembered that he had omitted to give her back her front door key.

A rhythmic scraping sound roused her.

It penetrated the warm, safe cocoon of darkness with a scrape-slither, scrape-slither that was almost a lullaby in itself, except that curiosity grew with growing awareness, and she had to find out the cause of the unidentifiable sound. She struggled out of the cocoon and discovered daylight filtering through the curtains. The darkness was caused by her head being under the bedclothes. She rubbed balled fists into her eyes, willing the last of the sleep daze away, and it was thus that Dom found her when he opened her bedroom door. Her curls were rumpled in wild dis- array, the tip of her tongue showed in a kitten yawn, and her cheeks were rosy with recently departed sleep. She looked about six years old. He said so, with a smile.

'You look about six years old.'

'I feel about sixty years younger that I did last night.' She felt fresh and alert, the numb exhaustion of the day be- fore dropped from her like a discarded cloak.

'It must be late.' She watched as Dom pulled aside the curtains and winter sun streamed through.

'It's after ten o'clock, but it doesn't matter, your Chief's given you the day off, so relax and eat your breakfast.'

He settled a loaded tray on her knees. There were crisp curls of bacon, a warm bread roll, more buttered toast, and a large mug of coffee.

'Eat up,' he bade her. 'I had mine ages ago.'

Margaret paused, with a curl of bacon poised precariously on her fork, and remembered last night. Remembered that he had not given her back her front door key. Had he...? Surely he had not stayed all night? She looked up at him, doubt and confusion struggling for supremacy in her face.

'The bread roll's still warm. I bought a bag of them from the baker on the way back here this morning,' he said casually.

So he had not stayed all night after all. Relief swept over her in a flood, and the bacon curl completed its journey without another pause. She bit into it with eager relish.

'By the way, here's your front door key.' He dropped it on to the tray beside the mug of coffee. 'I locked you in when I left last night, and took the key home with me, just in case someone decided to purloin your television set during the night,' he quipped. 'You were so sound asleep, you wouldn't have heard anyone removing your entire dining room furniture.'

'Something woke me.' It dawned on her that the peculiar scrape-slithering sound had stopped.

'Probably myself and the lads heaving that shingle into a tip-truck.' He sounded supremely casual.

'You mean some of the men from the rig?'

'One or two of them are on leave in the town, and they haven't got anything very important to do,' he said off-handedly. 'I alerted them that I'd need a bit of help to clear the pile from in front of your house—there's about a ton and a half of beach, if not more, right on your front doorstep,' he grimaced.

'Dom, you shouldn't ... I'd have coped, somehow. Oh, I wouldn't have shovelled it away myself, of course not,' at his derisive laugh, 'but the Council would have done it for me, I'm sure. You're on leave,' she remembered guiltily.

'I tried the Council first,' Dom disillusioned her, 'but apparently the shingle that's sitting on your doorstep is nothing but a molehill compared to the heap that's blocking the coast road between here and the next town. The Council's got its entire fleet of two bulldozers and every available workman slaving to get the traffic running again.'

They would have to, she realised with a sinking feeling of dismay. It was the only main road between Meldonmouth and the next town along the coast, and it carried a heavy weekday burden of commercial traffic that could not, because of its size, use the narrow twisting country lanes as an alternative.

'How long have the men been working outside?' She finished the rest of her breakfast with a haste it did not deserve. 'I'll get up, they'll want a break and a snack by now.'

'I've already given them one—bacon butties, and coffee. That's what's keeping them quiet now.'

And in his own break he had cooked her breakfast, instead of resting himself.

'I'll get up just the same, the least I can do is to cook them some lunch.'

'Better make it for just you and me, then,' Dom advised. 'We should be finished by about midday, and I heard the roustabouts planning to go back with the lorry driver. Don't embarrass them,' he stopped her protest, 'they want to get to the betting shop to place their stakes on the first race at Kempton, and they'll count your lunch poor return for a missed afternoon's sport,' he stated the bald truth. 'I'll attend to the men, leave them to me,' he told her, as if that closed the matter.

'I can hardly do that,' Margaret sparked angrily, resenting his calm appropriation of her responsibilities. 'It's my house,' she pointed out acidly, 'so presumably it's my pile of shingle outside as well. Would they accept a tip, do you think?' she about-faced, suddenly doubtful of her ability to cope with her sturdily independent helpers, whom Dom had so casually recruited without bothering to ask her first.

'They'll be mortally offended if you offer them one,' he warned, and his voice sharpened impatiently. 'I told you, leave them to me.'

He left her to carry her own tray downstairs, and a few

minutes later the scrape-slither that so obviously indicated shovels at work, now she knew what it was, started again with renewed vigour.

She ought to be glad the roustabouts would not be staying for lunch, she reflected, as she surveyed the contents of her fridge a few minutes later.

'Thank goodness the butcher delivered something before I went out the other day!'

Her own consumption of meat was small, her meals minute compared to the hearty helpings served on the rig, and because she catered for one, she kept little beyond immediate necessities, preferring to buy fresh and often. The steak, chops, kidney and sausage which would have kept her going for days would just make a decent sized grill for herself and Dom, she decided. She prayed he had not used all the bacon.

'It's still all here?' She looked at her own supply with a puzzled frown. Dom must have brought more in, along with the bread rolls. By his actions he had placed her under a further obligation to him, she thought vexedly, resenting the position into which she was forced through no fault of her own. She shrugged. She would cook him his lunch, and count that as adequate repayment. That, and the hospitality at the party on Sunday. She concentrated on the lunch. She did not particularly want to think about Sunday.

'The lads said to tell you cheerio.'

She jumped violently as Dom's voice spoke in her ear and the grill pan clattered alarmingly against the stove, hazarding its contents.

'Steady!' Dom grinned, and took it from her nerveless fingers. 'Life on an oil rig doesn't suit you,' he jibed, 'it's left you nervy.'

'Oh, don't be ridiculous,' she snapped, and snatched the pan back from him. 'Why didn't you tell me the men were leaving? I could at least have gone out and thanked them.' Mortification at what she felt convinced they would regard as bad manners on her part rose and choked her.

'They didn't want me to,' he retorted crisply. 'If they'd waited to listen to your speech of gratitude, they'd have missed the timing for the last bets on their race. So they said to tell you ....'

'Well, you've told me,' she snapped ungraciously, and sucked at her knuckle where it caught on the red-hot edge of the grill.

'There's no need to cook yourself as well,' Dom commented mildly, 'the grill looks to be plenty as it is. It smells good, too,' he sniffed hungrily.

'It's ready as soon as you are.' Being angry was no justification for letting the dinner spoil.

'Let's say now,' he retorted promptly, and began to soap his hands at the sink.

'Make yourself at home,' she invited sarcastically, and he grinned.

'I am,' he returned calmly, and reached for the towel hanging behind the door. 'This is much nicer than eating in a crowd.' He eyed the table set for two with undisguised satisfaction.

'You're impossible!' A sudden laugh surprised her irritation away. 'I do believe you sent the roustabouts away on purpose,' she accused him.

'I may have given them an incentive.' He did not look in the least guilty at the admission.

'If you've paid them, I'll pay you back.' Margaret frowned. She refused to be in Dom's debt for money, as well as the work of clearing the shingle. To be under an obligation to him at all was quite bad enough.

'Payments come in two varieties,' he said softly, adding, as she raised startled, questioning eyes, 'they can be made in cash—or kind.'

'Kind? Like what?' she asked sharply, and immediately regretted asking. Hurriedly she busied herself with dishing out the cooked meats, hoping he would not answer. She felt her colour rise, betraying the sudden, rapid beating of her heart.

'Like. . . .' He paused, his eyes watching her, and she gripped the handle of the grill pan convulsively, holding on to it as if it was a lifeline, to prevent her from sinking helplessly into the depths of their startling blue. 'Like—a mixed grill, shall we say, before it gets cold?'

He was laughing at her, and she hated him for it. She felt an almost irresistible urge to hurl the grill pan and its contents at his head. And then the thought of the empty fridge behind her stayed her hand, or she would go hungry as well as Dom. She did not care about Dom, she thought wrathfully, but empty pangs inside her warned her she had better care about herself.

'There's someone at your door.' The noise distracted him, and Margaret heaved an inaudible sigh of relief as his eyes turned away from her, towards the hall.

'It's the newspaper,' she interpreted the familiar household sounds. Perhaps Dom would go and fetch it, and leave her to dish up the meat in peace. Her hands shook in the most disconcerting manner while he watched her, and the fork clattered a castanet tattoo against the side of the grill pan that would surely draw a mocking comment from him soon. Her stomach curled in a tight knot, defensive against the mockery, even before it came, willing him to go away and fetch the newspaper.

'You get your paper late. Are you at the end of the round?'

'It comes before breakfast as a rule,' she answered indifferently. Why didn't he make a move towards the hall? Her nerves screamed with impatience at his slowness. 'It's been delayed by the storm, I expect, the papers come by road from the wholesaler in the town along the coast.' Which meant that the Council men must have bulldozed a way through, at least on the one side of the road, she realised.

'In that case, the Council's efforts mustn't be wasted.'

Dom latched on to her thoughts with his usual ease, and strolled into the hall. Margaret heard the letter box click back into place as he pulled the paper from it, and his foosteps started back again towards the kitchen. Then they stopped.

'Don't let the grill go cold,' she called out, throwing his own jibe back at him. He had probably stopped to check on the racing fixtures at Kempton. Really, he was as bad as the roustabouts, she thought, with every cook's vexation at having a perfectly cooked meal kept waiting.

'Has the storm made headlines?' She was not really interested. She put his filled plate down and indicated to him to take his place opposite to her.

'It has.' His voice was curt, and she looked up at him in surprise. His face had tightened, his expression closed in, remote from her, and he took his place at the table in silence. As he passed her place to take his chair he laid the paper front page up on the table beside her. The headlines leapt at her in large, bold black print.

'Heroine of the storm. Woman doctor braves gale to succour injured on oil rig,' they said.

CHAPTER TWELVE

LUNCH was a fraught meal. The newspaper headlines lay like a barrier between them. Glory-seeking. . . .

Against her will, Margaret's eyes kept straying to the print. It was all there, even the fact that she had joked with the M.O. about the dangers of hang-gliding. That, at least, gave her a clue as to the author of her present embarrassment. She recalled the young medico's enthusiastic, 'You've been absolutely fabulous!' And then he kissed her. And Dom had looked on, glowering, exactly as he glowered at her now from across the table. His scowl turned the grill into dust and ashes in her mouth. She plodded through it, hardly tasting what she ate, keeping her eyes on the paper.

The print seemed unaccountably blurred, and she blinked to clear her vision and doggedly read on. Most of the rest of the article consisted of a blow-by-blow account of the damage caused by the storm. It appeared to be considerable and widespread, even in an area noted for its storms, but the havoc it created along the coastline was as nothing compared to the havoc it had created in her life, she thought bitterly.

'The newspaper report isn't my fault. I didn't give them the story.'

She couldn't stand the strain any longer. Her fork clattered on to her plate, and she thrust her scarcely touched meal from her in an excess of exasperation.

'I know you didn't,' Dom replied evenly, and helped himself to another roll. 'I was here when you went to sleep last night,' he buttered it with meticulous care, 'and I was here when you woke up this morning, so you had no chance to give them the story.' He bit into the roll with crunchy precision.

'Are you suggesting that if you hadn't been with me, I should have grabbed the first opportunity of selling the story of my experiences to the newspapers?' she cried angrily. 'I've got better things to do,' she assured him scornfully. 'Like clearing away, when you've finished eating,' she added inhospitably.

'I've finished.' He sent her an even glance across the table, and demolished the last of his bread roll without answering her question.

'Have another coffee?' Remorse caught up with her belatedly. She did not usually treat her guests in such a cavalier fashion.

'We haven't got time.' He reached out and took her plate, stacking it on top of his own with a critical glance at the mostly untouched meal.

'We haven't?' She had plenty of time. As soon as Dom

was gone she intended to clear away the dishes and wash her hair. It felt sticky from its salt water wetting.

'We haven't,' he confirmed gravely. 'It's now,' he consulted his watch, 'half way through the afternoon. By the time we've cleared away and washed up, there'll be another half hour gone by, and you need to do some shopping. In case you hadn't noticed, I've just eaten you out of house and home,' he pointed out drily.

Most men would not have given it a second thought. And it was useless for her to deny it, the evidence was there in front of his eyes. She opened the fridge door and slid the butter dish inside. Its only companions were a single bottle of milk and the container of cheese.

'You're almost out of cornflakes, too, and I've just eaten the last bread roll.'

Dom watched pride and realism struggle for mastery in her face, and added pressure remorselessly on the side of realism. 'It's early closing day tomorrow, as well. I checked.'

He seemed to have thought of everything. 'That's the trouble with shopping at supermarkets,' Margaret said bitterly, out loud. 'You can't just ring them up and ask them to deliver the same as last week.' Her tone said how much she regretted the fact, and she tried to ignore the grin that lifted his lips and set him whistling cheerfully as he wiped the last of the crocks dry and stacked them neatly ready for her to put away.

'You know best where they go,' he acknowledged. For once, he admitted someone else knew best, she thought with incredulous sarcasm.

'You wiped those as if you'd had plenty of practice,' she could not forbear to jibe, and his grin widened.

'I lodged with Joy and Lex for a while, when we were testing an area for oil out East, and I wasn't allowed to get away with a thing,' he smiled. 'Joy did the cooking, and Lex and I had to do the washing up. No washing up, no next meal,' he remembered ruefully. 'Joy had us both well trained.'

'Good for Joy,' Margaret applauded, and hid her surprise with difficulty. In spite of Dom's protestations that he had no time for encumbrances, he fitted remarkably easily into a domestic role.

I should be used to him doing the unpredictable by now, she told herself.

'What did you say?' He fitted the grill pan back into its place, and raised enquiring eyes in her direction.

'Nothing.' She must have spoken out loud without realising it. Perhaps betrayed to Dom that she was thinking about him. 'I was thinking out loud, that's all,' she excused her lapse hastily.

'What about?' he asked interestedly, and his eyes held a mischievous gleam that brought the ready colour to her cheeks.

'Er—nothing,' she prevaricated. 'Well, the shopping, of course,' that was partly true, anyway. 'And about the party on Sunday.' Bringing Joy's name into the conversation reminded her about the party on Sunday. She must decide what to get for it, and quickly. When she so glibly issued the invitation, she did not bargain on being marooned on an oil rig for two whole days. Dom's reminder that it was early closing day tomorrow forced her to fix her mind on the need to feed six guests as well as herself. The experiences of the last two days had driven all thoughts of the party from her mind, she had not had time to think about provisions, let alone shop for them.

'Why not get your supplies while the car's available?' he suggested reasonably. 'We can put the lot in the trunk and bring it all back in one journey, then you won't have to worry about it if you go to the hospital tomorrow.'

It was the sensible thing to do. That was what made it so infuriating. Margaret felt driven into a corner, and her temper flared. It was not helped by the amused 'I told you so' expression on his face.

'Oh, come on, then, or the shops will be closed.' They would not. There was another hour and a half to go yet, but action helped. She fled round the house, grabbing her coat, shopping bags, and handbag. If Dom insisted on dragging her out shopping, she fumed, he could carry the shopping bags for her.

She banged the front door behind them unnecessarily hard. This time, she had got the front door key in her handbag. The thought gave her angry satisfaction. And then her annoyance melted and remorse rose up in her. The huge pile of shingle that blocked her entrance, as high as the eaves last night, had completely disappeared. Not only that, but the frontage was neatly swept free from sand and debris as if the storm had never existed.

'Are you sure about the shopping?' She paused doubtfully. 'All that shingle—you must be tired.' Dom had done his share of the shovelling, along with the roustabouts.

'Don't women ever make up their minds for two minutes together?' It was his turn to be impatient now. 'Get in, and don't argue,' he ordered her brusquely, and took the shopping bags from her, dumping them into the trunk of the car and shutting the door on her with a reflection of the front door's bang. He started the car amid a tense silence.

'You needn't get out,' she told him in a tight voice as he drew up outside the butcher's shop. 'I'm only going to drop my order in, he'll deliver it tomorrow morning.' That, at least, she need not bother him with, she thought defiantly.

'I wanted to know what we're eating on Sunday.' He sounded oddly plaintive, and she shot him a surprised look.

'Turkey,' she told him shortly. 'It's still near enough to Christmas to make it a seasonal lunch.' It was expediency, really. It saved her from having to think up a more complicated menu. A small turkey would cut up generously for six people, and be something the child would enjoy as well.

'That'll be great!' His enthusiastic exclamation tilted her lips in a reluctant smile.

'Do you like turkey all that much?' she asked him curiously. He enjoyed his food with the pure enjoyment of healthy hunger, but she had not noticed during the meals they ate together that he showed any signs of making a fetish of it, his spare frame denied him being a gourmet.

'It isn't only the turkey,' he replied seriously. 'It's having a Christmas dinner. Joy and Lex will enjoy it, too. We missed our Christmas this year,' he explained, and added at her enquiring look, 'We spent it in an airport transit lounge, marooned for three days by an engine failure and a blizzard. It was pretty desolate,' he remembered gloomily.

'You could have made up for it afterwards.' Suddenly sympathy caught Margaret unawares. No one should miss Christmas. Her own had been spent as usual at the hospital, working to keep her patients happy, but she had been with people she knew and liked. An airport transit lounge sounded bleak.

'We didn't have time to make up for it afterwards. We had to come here and start prospecting all over again.'

His voice was strangely wistful, and she glanced at him sharply. Was this another facet of the outwardly self-sufficient geologist? she wondered. Perhaps—she had a momentary flash of insight—perhaps it was his Achilles heel. Everyone was supposed to have one. She remembered his remark when he brought her two hot water bottles. 'We always had two, when we were small.' He spoke as if he might be one of a large family. Perhaps he missed the traditional family celebrations.

'You shall have your Christmas,' she promised impulsively, and felt oddly rewarded by a quick flash of pleasure that lit his eyes.

'Turkey, plum puddings. Everything except crackers,' she warned him. 'With Teddy around, I'm not going to risk crackers. We'll have balloons instead.'

'I'll blow them up for you,' he offered promptly.

'Only if you promise to use the balloon blower-up-er,' she cautioned. 'I'm not having anyone burst a blood vessel blowing up balloons for my party,' she put on her best 'Doctor Warrender' voice.

'I'll use your blower-up-er,' he promised meekly.

'In that case....' She relented, and they smiled at one another, for once in accord. And suddenly it was not her party any longer, it was their party. And she did not mind. An hour ago she would have resented it bitterly.

'Didn't you get the meat I sent you, Doctor?' The butcher regarded her unusual midweek appearance with some concern.

'Yes, but I used it for an unexpected visitor,' Margaret put his mind at rest. 'I need some more now, for a party on Sunday. I thought a turkey would be nice.'

'I'll go and find the balloons,' Dom said casually, and left her to her ordering.

'I shan't be a minute.'

But he did not seem to hear her. He strolled away, past the baker's shop where he bought the hot rolls for their breakfast, towards where the paper shop that sold the balloons stood at the top of the street next to the jewellers. He must have had to wait to be served, the same as she had, she guessed, because he was only just returning when she eventually escaped the friendly chatter of the butcher's assistant and made her way back to the car.

'Did you get your turkey?'

'Did you get your balloons?'

Suddenly they were laughing together, all traces of the previous tension vanished. Dom reached inside the trunk and scooped up her shopping bags.

'Let's get the groceries,' he commanded gaily, and tucked her hand through his arm. 'Teddy likes red jelly. No other colour will do.'

'Then red jelly he must have!'

They raided the supermarket shelves like two excited children.

'Tangerines?' He held up a tin enquiringly.

'Not tinned ones.' Margaret shook her head firmly. She had definite priorities where children were concerned, and guessed Joy would have, too. 'Fresh ones, from the greengrocer,' she insisted. 'And fresh herbs for the stuffing.' The turkey that had seemed an easy way out at first now turned into something special, and only the best would do.

They got their fresh tangerines, and sprigs of thymne and parsley, and more besides. Margaret bought sharp green apples, and dark bluish grapes, and Dom added delicate young apricots and a spiky fresh pinapple for good measure, and laughed when she scolded him for extravagance.

'How's your roof?' Margaret asked the greengrocer when they paid their reckoning, and at Dom's questioning look she told him about the slates and the accident on Monday morning.

'It's safe enough now, they've all been nailed back.' The shopkeeper saw Dom's wary upward glance as they emerged from the shop. 'Though it gave Doctor Warrender some unexpected work, I'm afraid.'

'Monday was quite a day,' Margaret agreed drily, and quickly changed the subject. She did not want the tension to rise between them again. Nothing must spoil the easy closeness that had flowered between them in the last carefree hour.

'It's surprising how quickly the storm's subsided.' Dom did not pursue the subject of Monday, and Margaret breathed a small sigh of relief. She let him take the groceries from her and fit them into the trunk of the car, then stood beside him, gazing out over the bay. 'To look at the sea now, you'd never believe what it was like twenty-four hours ago,' he remarked, but his expression was indifferent, not bothered by what had happened twenty-four hours ago. His voice was as quiet as the pre-evening calm that mantled the bay, spreading a tranquillity that made yesterday's widespread damage almost unbelievable.

'The area's known for its sudden storms.' Margaret accepted the vagaries of that particular stretch of coastline with a local's philosophy. 'They erupt without warning, but they die down just as quickly. Though they're savage while they last.'

That could well describe her relationship with Dom, she thought ruefully. When the storms flared between them she stood right in their path, as defenceless as the oil rig. She shivered, suddenly cold, and he stirred and glanced down at her.

'Let's go home and blow up the balloons.' He tucked her into the car, and this time he did not slam the door.

She sorted out her own key when they reached the cottage. Dom waited beside her, his arms full of parcels, and she pushed open the door and turned, intending to take one from him to relieve his load.

'They're evenly balanced,' he refused her, 'though they seem heavier than the armful I carried into the house last night,' he grinned. 'Or perhaps they've just got more sharp angles.' His eyes teased her, holding the memory of her in his arms the night before.

'Be thankful you haven't got a pile of shingle to climb over this time.' She made a difficulty of removing the key from the lock, suddenly confused, unable to meet his eyes.

'I've got a bag that's going to spill any minute, unless I find somewhere to put it down,' he warned her, and she pulled the key hurriedly into her hands and led the way inside.

'Put them on the table.' She slid out the support for the extra leaf and he eased his burden down on to it.

'If you put the kettle on, I'll put the groceries away.'

She turned her back on him, glad to shield her face, but at the same time aware of his every movement, aware of the splashing water as he filled the kettle, the sudden hot hiss of the gas. She emptied the first bag of parcels and turned to start on the second.

'Mind, it's slipping!'

They both grabbed for the packet of red jelly that slid off the top of the pile, and upended tantalisingly right on the edge of the table.

'I've got it!'

'No, I have.'

They caught the packet, and one another's fingers, at the same time.

'It's mine!'

'Not unless you pay a forfeit.' Dom kept hold of the packet, and with his other hand he held on to her fingers, drawing her close to him. 'We always played forfeits at Christmas.' He held the packet high over her head, tantalising her.

'It isn't the party yet. Not until Sunday.' Margaret's eyes flashed upwards, calculating her chances of reaching the packet of jelly. They were nil, his arm was too long for her to hope to reach it. His lips hovered above her own, and she turned her face sideways, defying him, refusing to give in.

'A forfeit?' he demanded softly, and his lips caressed the tip of her ear.

'No! I told you, it isn't the party yet.' Her protest trailed off weakly. She could not continue to defy him, if he held her close like this, her pulses raced with his nearness.

'Didn't you ever dip your finger into the trifle, for a taste before the party?' She felt his silent laughter, mocking her.

'N-never.'

'You're telling fibs,' he accused her, and punished her by leaving a trail of fire with his lips across her soft, averted cheek. Defeated, she half turned towards him, her leaping pulses clamouring to respond, her arms starting to rise, to clasp his head and draw his mouth down over her own, to savour the full, heady sweetness of his kiss. And then the kettle whistled.

'The kettle's boiling.'

'... the kettle!'

His voice was muffled. His arm dropped, his fingers let go of the packet of jelly, and it fell back on to the table with a flaccid thud, within reach of her hand, but her hand was no longer interested in the jelly. It was fully occupied in relishing the feel of crisp, blond, wavy hair beneath her fingers, tamed to neatness against a strong, sunburned neck.

'Oh, do be quiet!' Dom exclaimed at last, and lifted his head in exasperation. No sound can be more destructive to romance than the whistle of a boiling kettle. Only nostalgia, and the dimming kindliness of distant memory, can soften the strident 'wheep' to acceptable limits. The kettle whistled on, shrilly demanding attention, and sudden laughter surfaced inside Margaret. She remembered the jelly. Deftly she captured it, and slid it into the cupboard.

'You haven't paid your forfeit.'

Dom saw her movement and rounded on her, his hand hovering over the kettle handle.

'I have,' she protested, but halfheartedly. 'Forfeits only have to be paid once.' She would not mind paying it again, over and over again if necessary. Rose colour stained her cheeks, and of a sudden gold-tipped lashes veiled her eyes, lest he should see how little she would mind. Her heart thudded with slow, painful strokes.

'Red jelly carries a double forfeit,' he insisted, 'it's special....' His hand hovered closer to the kettle, and sparked a warning in her mind.

'Use the kettle-holder,' she exclaimed urgently.

'Ouch! That was hot.' His hand descended on the handle even as she spoke, too late to prevent him from grasping it.

'I told you to use the kettle-holder.' The precious minute between them was destroyed.

'You can dress the burn for me,' he offered it back to her again.

'Hold your hand under the cold tap. That'll be sufficient to stop it from stinging.' It had not blistered, she could see that. And even if it had, she did not trust herself to treat it for him. Dared not trust herself to touch him. Contact with

Dom was like contact with a flash of lightning. It burned her armour, reduced her resistance to ashes, and filled her with unnamed longings that crystallised all that her life had held until she met him—and faced her with its emptiness. And offered the promise of what could be, if only. . . .

But Dom travelled alone, without encumbrances. He had made a point of telling her so himself, when they first met, and the memory turned the swift beating of her heart into a leaden weight within her breast. It dimmed the brightness of the afternoon that lay behind them, and the party that was to come, and made her voice flat with dark depression as she said,

'Let's have our cup of tea. I'm thirsty.' And dared not add that the thirst, like the hunger, was for him. . . .

CHAPTER THIRTEEN

DOM did not comment on her sudden change of mood. He looked at her, a long, probing look that asked a silent question, and must have found an answer in her closed expression and averted eyes, because he shrugged indifferently, accepting that the moment was over, and she did not want it back.

'I do! I do!'

Margaret's heart—her whole being—cried otherwise, yearning for the feel of his arms again, for the touch of his lips. But her mind held her back, cautioning her. Hearts were not playthings, to be tossed to the rending claws of a wildcat, she told herself bitterly; objects to be toyed with for a moment, and then left barren and bleeding when the game was over, and Dom was tired of the play.

Silently she handed him the tea caddy, watched while he spooned dark leaves into the pot and poured on the boiling water. He used the kettle-holder this time. It was red, like the hot water bottle covers, knitted spoils from a local sale of work. Margaret's eyes registered the familiar objects dispassionately. The silence seemed loud in her ears now that the kettle had stopped whistling. Almost she missed the noise and wished it would continue. There was nothing to say between them while the tea brewed, and the kettle had used up the silence, which stretched now through an endless space of emptiness that seemed to her taut nerves to go on and on.

'One lump, or two?'

'None for me, thank you.'

The polite exchange of banalities only served to make the silence worse, underlining it. The cosy intimacy which had lain between them was fled.

'I'll blow up the balloons, while you put the rest of the groceries away.'

'Use this.' She reached out the gaily coloured balloon pump, and Dom took it from her without comment.

'Where do you want them put, when they're blown up?'

'In the living room.' She carried on sorting the groceries. She did not offer to show him where the living room was. If he wanted to blow up the balloons in there, it was up to him. Out of the corner of her eye she watched him open the living room door and disappear through it. He did not seem to have any trouble finding it, she thought tartly, then justice reminded her that there was only one other door he could go through. She lived in a cottage, not a mansion. Sudden tears stung her eyes. 'He'd rather be in the living room on his own than in here with me,' she thought miserably. His move away from her seemed to confirm his antipathy to encumbrances, his determination to avoid becoming entangled. . . .

'I hope to goodness he won't try to blow up all those balloons with his mouth.' He might, simply because she had asked him not to. The doctor in her came uppermost, and she opened her mouth to call through to him, then through the partly opened door came the faint puff-clop, puff-clop of the balloon pump, vigorously wielded. A loud bang followed on the heels of the umpteenth puff-clop, and a muttered imprecation floated to her ears. She giggled.

'That'll teach him not to use the same roughshod methods with balloons as he does with people,' she muttered maliciously. 'They don't take kindly to it, either.'

A short pause followed, and she listened intently, then the puff-clops continued, with rather less vigour than before, and there were no more bangs.

'He's learned his lesson.' She gave a grin of satisfaction, then it faded, and her lips drooped. Had she learned her own lesson? she wondered bleakly. The homily on caution delivered by her mind seemed to have no effect at all on her feelings. They felt as raw as her nerves. She dropped a packet of butter from suddenly paralysed fingers when Dom spoke from the doorway.

'I've piled all the balloons on to the settee, ready for when you want them.'

He did not offer to help her put them up, and disappointment pierced her, irrational disappointment, because it was her own withdrawal that had rebuffed him, not the other way round. He had merely accepted the rebuff, and with feminine lack of logic she resented his easy acceptance. She felt him watching her, and stubbornly she kept her eyes on the last of the groceries in her hands, placing them carefully on the shelves, as if ranging them in size order was the most important thing in her life. If she looked at him he might read the disappointment and the resentment in her face.

He waited for a moment or two, then, when she did not respond he reached out and picked up his jacket from where he had slung it across the back of a chair when they came in. He shrugged into it with a quick movement of his shoulders.

'See you.'

With a laconic wave of his hand that reminded Margaret irresistibly of the roustabout's ultra-casual leavetaking, Dom turned on his heel and left her. She stared for a min-

ute or two at the closed door, unable to take in the fact that
he had gone. The slam of the car door broke her trance,
and she ran to the window, in time to see the tail lights disappear round the curve of the harbour wall. She turned
back from the window on dragging feet, through the empty
silence of the room that mocked the empty desolation of
her heart. He had gone. And he had not said goodnight.
Had not kissed her goodnight, she meant, but she would
not allow herself even to think it. She put up her hand
wearily to brush away an errant curl that insisted on coming
out of place, and found her cheeks were wet.

There was no one there to see the tears, and she made
no attempt to check them. The loneliness, and the desolation, flowed from her as they had done on the rig, and with
the same result, so that when in desperation she turned up
at the hospital the next morning, in the hope that work
might stem the unresolved circle of question and answer
that went round and round in her mind through the endless
hours of the sleepless night, her white face and darkly
shadowed eyes drew comment, first of all from Bill Quinn,
and then from her returned Chief.

'You look ghastly,' said Bill with unflattering bluntness.

'You still don't look fully rested.' Neil Venables was
politer, but his gaze was no less searching. 'Stay and do
your ward rounds if you want to satisfy yourself that we've
looked after your patients properly,' he smiled, miscon-
struing her motive in a way that made Margaret feel instantly guilty. Her reason for coming to work this morning
was purely selfish.

'You know I don't. . . .' she began to protest, and her
Chief laughed.

'I know,' he said soothingly, 'we're all as bad as one another in this profession. My wife calls it work mania. But
while you're here, it'll be a good opportunity for you to
meet the new man who came from London with me.'

'He's already getting himself established. He's a sound
chap,' Bill Quinn pronounced, after Margaret had been

introduced, and voiced her approval of Neil's choice to the house surgeon when he accompanied her on her ward rounds. 'I'm not making you feel superfluous, am I?' he grinned, and Margaret grimaced back at him.

'You're trying your best,' she retorted, then more seriously, 'I think we're lucky to get him, we could do with another of the same calibre. I've certainly got no quarrel with Neil's choice,' she assured Bill sincerely, 'though,' she paused at the foot of a bed as they entered a side ward, 'I've got a bone to pick with you,' she told the occupant sternly.

'Why me?' The young M.O. from the oil rig put down his magazine and looked up. It was another periodical on the subject of hang-gliding, she noticed. Its reader greeted her with a friendly grin.

'You were responsible for that wretched newspaper article,' Margaret accused him.

'I thought you deserved a pat on the back for what you did on the rig,' the instigator of the article acknowledged his guilt unrepentantly.

'I don't like that kind of publicity,' Margaret told him bluntly, 'it was journalese at its worst, and you know it. And I don't consider I deserved the embarrassment it caused me.' She made her disapproval plain.

'Gosh, I'm sorry, I didn't think.' He looked suitably crestfallen.

'You should have thought.' She was not inclined to give him any quarter, Dom's reaction to the newspaper headlines still stung. 'So if the reporters come back—no more heroics. Agreed?' she insisted, and relented slightly at his downcast nod. 'Or I might be inclined to retaliate—and not by a pat on the back,' she threatened significantly.

'I'll be a model of discretion,' he promised hastily. 'I don't want another of those injections like the last one you gave me. You were cruel.'

'She can be, when she's so inclined,' a voice agreed blandly, and Margaret spun round, her face aflame.

'It isn't visiting time yet,' she blurted out the first thing that came into her head. If it sounded unwelcoming, she could not help it. She did not feel like welcoming Dom. What was he doing here at this hour? She had felt so sure, when she came in to work this morning, that she would be safe from any accidental contact with him, at least until visiting hours, and then she planned to take clinic on purpose to avoid the possibility of bumping into him if he came to visit the wards. And now here he was beside her on her ward round, and accusing her of being cruel into the bargain. She glared at him furiously.

'Bill gave me carte blanche to come in and see the rig people whenever I pleased,' Dom countered. 'He said plenty of visitors would save them from getting bored, and I'm doing just that,' he pointed out smugly, and indicated the pile of books and periodicals he carried under his arm as if they were an official passport to the wards, Margaret thought angrily.

She bit back the heated words that rose to her lips. If Bill Quinn had given Dom permission to visit out of hours, there was nothing she could say. Her rank gave her the right to countermand such an instruction, but she knew she must not undermine Bill's authority, it would only incur his resentment to no good purpose. The whole situation was impossible, she thought wrathfully. There was no reason why the patients from the rig should not enjoy free visiting, they were none of them in a serious plight, and while they were confined to bed, boredom was indeed their worst enemy.

'If you continue to encourage him in this hang-gliding nonsense,' she said sourly at last, catching sight of the M.O.'s favourite magazine in the pile under Dom's arm, 'he's likely to spend a lot more of his time in hospital.'

'Hang-gliding's no more dangerous than an oil rig,' protested its devotee, 'and you braved the rig yourself, without turning a hair,' he reminded her slyly.

'Margaret only came out to you because I happened to be in theatre when the call came,' Bill laughed, and Margaret froze. She did not want Dom to know her reason for answering the call herself. It was nothing to do with him. She scowled a warning at Bill, but perversely he did not notice, and continued speaking to the M.O. 'If I'd been free at the time I'd have come out to the rig myself, which wouldn't have been half so interesting for you,' he teased.

Margaret felt Dom's look burn right through her back, even through the stiff starched whiteness of her hospital coat—the armour that should protect her, and no longer did. She dared not look round; she did not need to. She could feel the angry accusation in his look, demanding to know why she had not told him. Accusing her of holding back.

'I'm glad you were busy at the time,' the young M.O. told Bill with engaging frankness, 'it couldn't have been better, the way it was,' he gave Margaret a glance in which both mischief and appreciation showed plainly. 'And at least you've got your watch back,' he said to her more seriously. 'I'm glad you didn't lose it, after all.'

'My watch?' Margaret's frown turned from anger to puzzlement. 'But I haven't got it back, it went overboard.' The anger returned as she thought about the loss of her watch.

'That's funny,' it was the M.O.'s turn to look puzzled now, 'when the 'copter pilot came in this morning, he said one of the divers found your watch when they went down yesterday to see what damage the storm had done. Apparently the strap had got caught up on one of the rig anchor chains. The pilot asked me to tell you. I thought he said he'd given the watch to you, Dom?' he turned to the geologist. 'You were with a crowd of the roustabouts on a lorry, or something,' he said vaguely. 'The pilot said you told him you'd be seeing Margaret, so he handed you the watch to give to her, and save himself the journey.'

That would be when Dom was on his way to her house the previous morning, to clear the shingle. He must have had her watch in his pocket when he arrived. And he had said nothing about it to her. Her eyes flashed green fire, and she rounded on him angrily.

'You didn't say a word to me about having my watch,' she blazed. 'You kept it....'

'You didn't tell me the reason you came out to the rig yourself, instead of sending Bill,' he countered. 'Anyway,' he added offhandedly, 'your watch is treasure trove now.'

'It's nothing of the kind!' Anger drained the colour from her face, leaving it a deathly mask from which her eyes burned into his with emerald hostility. 'It's my property,' she cried, 'and I want it back.' She choked at his bland effrontery. 'Give it back to me this instant!' she demanded hotly.

'I haven't got it.' He returned her furious look with one that was ice-cool, and completely unperturbed. 'Treasure trove has to be handed in,' he pointed out, as if he was trying to reason with an obtuse child, she thought angrily.

With an effort, Margaret took a grip on herself. She had learned before, to her cost, that anger had no effect on this man. It was like throwing pebbles at a fortress. She spoke through stiff lips.

'Tell me where you've taken it, and I'll collect it myself.'

'I doubt if they'd hand it over to you.' He paused, frowning, as if he was giving the matter due consideration. 'The receipt's in my name, you see,' he said finally.

She stared at him, stunned into speechlessness. Drumbeats of impotent fury pulsed in her ears, and she drew breath with difficulty.

'I'll get it back,' she breathed. 'I'll get it back, if it's the last thing I do!' Her voice was a thin thread of sound, loud enough for Dom to hear, but not the others, and she faced him, a tiny, defiant figure, bristling with outrage, her head back-tilted to fling her challenge directly in his face. Fleetingly, an odd expression darkened the vivid blue of his eyes, then it was gone as a new voice spoke from the doorway.

'We seem to have half the oil rig staff spending their leave at the General.'

A tolerant smile lit Neil Venable's face, and he strolled

into the side ward to join them, accompanied, to Margaret's surprise, by Lex Noble. 'I heard your colleague here enquiring for you,' Neil told Dom, 'so I brought him along to join you. Now, if you'll excuse me. . . .' He took his leave of the little group with a courteous nod—and took the fierce tension along with him. Margaret drew a deep, shuddering breath. She felt drained, and faintly sick.

'I guessed you'd be here,' said Lex, 'that's why I came along.'

'What's your news?' She felt Dom stiffen, even as he asked. The moment Lex appeared, the geologist's whole attention switched from herself to the Jamaican, as if Lex's appearance was a portent of something she did not understand. It was like having a powerful torch shining in her eyes one minute, and switched off the next. Through a daze she heard Lex's deep drawl.

'No good news,' the drilling engineer replied. 'The divers went down as soon as the swell subsided sufficiently to make it safe. That's when they found your watch.' He flashed a smile at Margaret, and she smiled back weakly, praying he would not enlarge on the subject of her watch. She did not feel she could stand another wordy battle with Dom at the moment. To her relief Lex continued on the subject of the divers. 'They made a thorough inspection of the gear and came up with the news that the wellhead is badly damaged. You produce some good storms round here,' he told Margaret ruefully. 'And of course, the standby vessel ramming the rig didn't help much, either. One way and another, the storm and the vessel between them caused a lot of mischief at sea-bed level.'

'How soon can it be repaired before we start drilling again?'

Margaret could feel Dom's tension, it twanged like a too-tight instrument string, vibrating in waves between him and his colleague. He rocked slightly on the balls of his feet, awaiting Lex's answer, like a runner about to spring into action. Typically, she thought, he discounted the difficulties and problems of repairing the damage done by the storm. To him, difficulties were merely something to be overcome. Already, his mind leapt ahead to the crux of the whole operation—to drill, in search of oil.

'How soon?' Lex repeated thoughtfully. 'That's debatable.' The Jamaican's dark eyes measured his friend cautiously, and Margaret tensed. Lex's voice was charged with something more than just news of the damage. Dom knew it, too, the tautness of his lithe frame, the slight narrowing of the vivid eyes, all told of intense alertness—but to what danger? Her eyes flashed from one man to the other, trying to discover what it was that charged the atmosphere between them. Her own sensitive awareness, made more acute by her new awareness of Dom, told her that challenge was there, and defiant repudiation. But why?

'Repairs will come expensive,' Lex said laconically. He seemed to be trying to tell Dom something, to convince him, though of what she could not guess.

'Repairs are always expensive, in time as well as money.' The geologist's voice was flat. 'Give it to me straight,' he demanded harshly.

'If that's the way you want it....' Lex shrugged with seeming indifference, but Margaret noticed his glance held a depth of compassion as he faced his friend. She caught her breath, fearing she knew not what as he continued, 'A routine report went to the Board of Directors, giving an assessment of the damage, and the possible cost of repairs in time and money. Within the hour they sent a wireless instruction back to the rig to suspend all operations. They're calling an emergency Board meeting to consider whether to allow drilling to continue, or——' he paused, hesitated, then went on firmly, 'or seal the well, and abandon it.'

'That's one wildcat that's produced no kittens.' The young M.O. joined in the conversation with a flippant lack of tact that made Margaret long to hit him. She stole a glance at Dom. His face was white and set.

'Your career could be at stake over this. . . .'

Lex did not actually repeat his earlier warning, but it hung in the air between them like a banner, emphasised by the gravity of the Jamaican's silent regard.

It could ruin Dom. All that he had worked for. All that he was. The other two geologists would show no mercy in proving that they had been right and he had been wrong. In a flash her watch, the balloons, their quarrel—she could not even remember, now, how it had started—seemed unimportant. She turned impulsively and laid a hand on his arm.

'Dom. . . .'

'Never mind what instructions you've received from the Board.' His voice was harsh but, she noticed, perfectly controlled. He ignored her hand as if it was not there, yet he must have felt it on his arm, she saw him glance down as her fingers touched his sleeve. She withdrew them, pretending to fumble in her pocket for her handkerchief, which became suddenly necessary to hide the hurt of his rebuff.

'Get the repairs under way,' he demanded, 'and start the drills working again. There's oil in that basin, and we shan't reach it until we drill deep enough.'

'We've found no signs of hydrocarbons so far.' Lex's voice was expressionless, stating something they both already knew.

'There will be.' Dom sounded as positive as ever, and he took a step towards his friend. 'Do this for me, Lex,' he demanded. 'I know I'm right.'

Margaret held her breath. Even the young M.O. and Bill Quinn remained quiet, in the face of the silent drama being played out between the two professionals, the clash of loyalties between expertise and friendship.

'Do this for me, Lex. . . .'

Would he? Margaret wondered. Dom was asking a good deal of him. Not so much to get the rig working again as to defy the Board of the powerful oil combine that employed them both, throw in his lot with the geologist, thereby risking his job and jeopardising his future career. Putting his friendship to the ultimate test, Margaret thought critically, on the slender chance that Dom's judgment was sound, and two older, more experienced geologists were in the wrong.

Lex did not hesitate.

'I'll do it—for both of us.' The Jamaican's face suddenly split into a large grin. 'I've got a special reason of my own, as well,' he began mysteriously, then stopped. 'But never mind that now. Come on,' he grasped Dom's arm. 'We've got no time to waste. Let's get going!'

'Don't forget the party on Sunday,' Bill Quinn roused himself to call after the two as they made for the door.

'We'll be there, never fear,' Lex called back over his shoulder. 'You can help us to celebrate!' And he was gone, dragging Dom impatiently along with him.

'Help them to celebrate? I wonder....' Bill quirked a significant eyebrow at Margaret. The consequences of what the two rebels intended to do had not been lost on the house surgeon, either, she thought worriedly. 'More likely we'll be commiserating with them over a pair of wrecked careers,' he predicted gloomily.

CHAPTER FOURTEEN

IT was the longest day Margaret had ever known.

The clinic, which this morning offered the ideal refuge from Dom, now dragged endlessly. Children seemed more fractious than usual, grown-ups more inclined to talk. Or was it she who was less inclined to listen? she wondered remorsefully. Subconsciously her ears remained alert for the sound of Dom's returning footsteps. Among all the other feet that walked through the clinic entrance, she would instantly recognise his. But they did not come. By five o'clock the headache that had threatened since that morning became a throbbing reality.

'Have you heard from Dom since he left?' Bill Quinn strolled through the surgery door on the heels of the last departing patient and spoke without preamble.

'No, I don't expect to, really,' she answered. She had hoped that by some miracle Dom would allay her fears for his future, ring and tell her that he and Lex had decided not to go ahead with their mad scheme after all, and wait for the ruling of their Board.

But he did not ring! obviously he did not think she warranted being kept up to date with his news. Perhaps that was part of being an encumbrance, she thought bitterly. Someone to whom Dom would have to explain his actions. He could not consider her future lay with him, or that she might have any interest in his. The knowledge cut with the sharpness of one of her own surgical knives, and tears stopped her voice. 'No, I haven't heard.' She shook her head, unable to continue.

'They're a pair of madmen,' Bill complained. 'If the oil company gets wind of what they're doing, it won't be only their wildcat well that will be sealed off and abandoned,' he predicted ominously.

'I've discovered an advantage in being married to a doctor,' Sue announced, joining them as Bill spoke. 'At least he's never likely to be out of work!'

'Not unless I sew up someone back to front, because my mind's distracted by the resident therapist,' Bill retorted flippantly.

'Make sure you don't, because you'll soon add me to your responsibilities,' Sue quelled him. 'But I honestly don't see what you two are fretting about,' she pursued the subject that occupied all their minds. 'Boards don't hold meetings on oil rigs,' she pointed out practically, 'and unless someone tells tales and sends the Board a wireless message alerting them to what's going on, they won't know what Lex and Dom are doing until the repairs are finished and the drilling started again,' she said hopefully. 'By that time, they'll have struck oil,' she added dramatically, 'and once Dom's been proved right, they won't be able to say anything,' she finished with a sublime confidence which Margaret wished heartily she could share.

'It's the consequences of Dom being proved wrong that we're worrying about,' Bill gloomed.

'We should know one way or the other on Sunday,' Sue reasoned, 'we'll all be at Maggie's party together then, you'll just have to bide in patience a little longer.'

'It's more likely to turn into a wake, rather than a party, with the news Lex and Dom will bring with them.' The house surgeon was determined to look on the black side, and secretly Margaret agreed with him. More than ever she wished Neil had delayed his return so that she could postpone the party.

'I do wish you two would cheer up,' Sue grumbled. 'You'll make me begin to have doubts next!'

'I'm thinking about what Joy will say, when she knows what Dom's asked Lex to do,' Margaret confessed.

'She'll start divorce proceedings, I shouldn't wonder,' Bill prophesied darkly.

'Nothing of the kind,' Sue cried indignantly, 'she'll back Lex and Dom to the limit. I know Joy,' she stated unanswerably, 'she's got faith in them.'

Implying that she had not. Margaret flushed at the oblique criticism.

'I'm keeping my fingers crossed until Sunday, just the same,' she sidestepped the issue and rose to her feet, stretching wearily. 'As soon as I've finished writing up these records, I'm off home,' she announced. 'I've got lots to do for Sunday.' It was too early to start preparing anything yet for the party but it served as an adequate excuse. 'I'll be back in here again tomorrow.'

'So shall I,' Sue answered, 'but I've got all Saturday free. Bill's on duty, so I'll come along and give you a hand with the preparations then,' she offered generously. 'In the meantime, perhaps either Lex or Dom will call in and let us know what's happening.'

Her hope was unfounded. The following day, neither the geologist nor the drilling engineer put in an appearance. Several times Margaret made an excuse to pass through the side ward where the men from the rig were accommodated, but each time she was doomed to disappointment. Several of the rig staff came in during the day to visit the patients in the side ward. They included the helicopter pilot, who admitted cheerfully to, 'shunting the old bus backwards and forwards all day, what with one thing and another,' but she resisted the temptation to question him. One incautious word on her part might be enough to jeopardise the success of Dom's plan and run both men into trouble. Deliberately Margaret worked later than usual, willing her telephone to ring, but perversely for once the usually busy instrument remained silent. At last she put on her coat just as the night staff came on duty.

'Any snags, doctor?'

'No, nothing special to watch out for,' she responded automatically. 'I just stayed on to finish some report writing,' she used the bugbear of every doctor as an excuse, and made her way disconsolately outside. Already, she noticed, the daylight was beginning to lengthen. February had given way to March, and a subtle difference tinged the air. Spring trod on the heels of winter, hidden still, but indefinably there. But instead of its bringing its usual uplift to her spirits, a wave of depression closed over her. She wished she had never suggested a Christmas party.

'It was a silly idea.'

She spoke aloud to herself, bitterly regretting the mistaken impulse that prompted the idea in the first place. The helicopter droned by overhead. Her ears caught the familiar rattle, but this time she did not bother to look up. Dom would not be in the machine. There would only be the pilot on the last of his 'shunts' for the day. Probably taking spares out to the rig, to where Lex and Dom toiled to get the drills working again.

The brightly coloured balloons mocked her as she opened the living room door, and she closed it again dispiritedly. She would put them up tomorrow. She wondered if, after all, they would be needed. Lex and Dom might still be working on the rig; working desperately, against time. And if they were not, if their rebel bid had failed, then Joy might not want to come. Bill and Sue would come, but two people did not constitute a party. But the therapist herself appeared to harbour no such misgivings when she arrived early the next morning, before Margaret had finished her breakfast.

'I'll join you in a cup of coffee.' Sue helped herself from the percolator. 'As soon as we've washed up, we can start on the preparation work. I'm looking forward to tomorrow,' she smiled.

'I was just wondering if we're wasting out time,' Margaret spoke her doubts out loud, unable to share her companion's zest.

'Of course we're not!' The other girl looked at her in astonishment. 'Whatever makes you think that?'

'Lex and Dom might still be on the rig, struggling to repair the damage, instead of coming to the party,' Margaret pointed out.

'They'll be finished by tonight, however bad the damage is—surely it's only a matter of getting spares? Once they're exchanged for the damaged bits, hey presto!' Sue waved her coffee cup, to its mortal danger, 'they can start drilling again.'

'I hope it's as simple as that,' Margaret responded fervently. She had little taste for her own coffee. 'If they fail. . . .' She left the sentence unfinished.

'If they fail, they'll both get a rocket from their Board,' Sue admitted ungrammatically. 'Not just Dom. Lex will get into trouble as well.'

'I know, but it'll be worse for Dom.'

'I don't see. . .?'

'Because Dom asked Lex to take the risk for him,' Margaret begged her understanding. 'If things go wrong, he'll not only ruin his own career, he'll have to bear the burden of knowing he's brought Lex down with him too.' She did not add the rest of her fears. Remorse could destroy a sensitive, finely tuned mind like Dom's. It could ruin a life, as well as a career.

'You love Dom, don't you?'

Sue's candid eyes met Margaret's in a straight look, and in them was a wealth of sympathy and understanding.

'Is it as obvious as all that?' Margaret was dismayed by the unexpected statement. It was a statement, not a question, and she did not trouble to deny it.

'Plain as a pikestaff,' Sue retorted cheerfully. 'But don't worry,' she comforted, 'its probably only because I'm in love myself that I guessed how it was with you. It's fellow feeling,' she grinned, then sobered. 'I think I should die with worry, if things were going as wrong for Bill as they are for Dom,' she confessed. 'They're serious, aren't they?'

'Very,' Margaret retorted crisply, 'but there's nothing you and I can do about it, except hope they right themselves.'

She got up from the table determinedly. In the face of Sue's sudden drop in spirits, her own rallied to strengthen them both. 'Maybe we'll know tomorrow, one way or the other, and by that time we shall want a super meal prepared, to either celebrate with, or act as a consolation.'

'That looks gay enough to make up for any number of missed Christmasses.' Sue collapsed on to the settee several hectic hours later, and lay back limply. 'Heavens!' She sat up again hurriedly. 'I've just found the one balloon we forgot to hang up.' She eyed the brightly decorated picture rail. 'There isn't an inch of room to fit another one in.'

'Leave it.' Margaret subsided thankfully beside her. 'Teddy will want a loose balloon to play with.'

'I hope that young imp appreciates the trouble we've

gone to on his behalf,' Sue groaned wearily.

'He won't,' Margaret laughed, 'but he'll enjoy his red jelly, and the iced sponge with the cherries on top.' She tried not to remember how she and Dom had tussled for the packet of red jelly; of how he held her, and the forfeit he had demanded—and taken. If she had not withdrawn, how would it have ended? she wondered. Would Dom have told her he loved her? But she had withdrawn, and she would never know.

'Would you like something to eat? It's long past tea-time.' She got to her feet again abruptly. To rest was to think, and to think was dangerous.

'Not for me, thanks,' Sue was adamant. 'I've seen enough of food for one day. After helping you prepare turkey and trimmings, trifle, cake and jelly, the only thing that could tempt me now would be a crust of bread and a piece of sharp cheese—and that not until I've been home and prettied myself up ready for tomorrow. I'll come early and help you with the table,' she offered. 'The things we've made today look tempting enough to make any party go with a swing,' she declared contentedly.

This was one party that would not.

Margaret knew it with a sinking heart the moment her guests arrived on the front doorstep the next morning. Joy did her best to assume a surface gaiety, but nothing could erase the look of strain from her fine dark eyes. Her deter-minedly bright smile somehow never quite managed to reach them.

'We've come with good appetites,' Lex declared, sniffing the aroma of done-to-a-turn turkey with an appreciative nose, but when it came to actually eating his share, he wielded his knife and fork with an abstracted air, as if he did not really notice what it was on his plate. Joy's sense of strain was accentuated in the two oil men, fine-honed with the tension of unspoken dissent, and betrayed by sudden silences that dropped like vacuums amid the conversation, and made the subdued clink of cutlery seem inordinately loud. It stretched Margaret's nerves to screaming point by the end of the second course. Even Sue, she noticed, was unusually silent, probably because her knowledge of the state of Margaret's feelings made her react to the atmosphere more strongly than she would otherwise have done.

Dom greeted Margaret gravely when he first arrived, but with Teddy chattering excitedly, and the others all talking at once, his aloof manner passed unnoticed by everyone except Margaret. Perhaps it was only her imagination that made him appear distant, as it could have been coincidence that made him seem to avoid her when they all went indoors. And when it came time to sit down to their meal, Dom took his place without comment at the other end of the table, between Sue and Joy, leaving the chair next to her own empty, for Bill to occupy when he came in bearing the turkey in triumph. Margaret regarded her party unhappily. Under the surface cheer lurked a brittle tension that felt as if it might snap at any moment. Only Bill and Teddy seemed unaffected by the cross-currents of feeling that surged round them.

'He likes me, after all,' the house surgeon discovered jubilantly as the toddler responded happily to his tentative advances with the spare balloon.

'It wasn't you he disliked before,' Joy smiled, 'it was your white coat.'

'It scared him off,' said Dom, and somehow, although he spoke to Bill, his eyes found Margaret's across the room, and in them was a wealth of meaning. She stirred uneasily in her chair, resenting the undertone of accusation in his voice. Her white coat—her armour—had not deterred him, she thought resentfully. He had managed to penetrate it the first time they met, and behaved as if it did not exist ever since. It was a relief when Bill took charge after the meal was over and shooed herself and Sue out of the kitchen.

'You two made the meal for us, so we'll do the washing up.' He stepped aside for Dom and Lex, who followed him burdened with an armful of plates each.

'I didn't help with any of the preparations,' Joy protested, but she sounded halfhearted, and Margaret glanced across at her, surprised. The last time they had met she had seemed to be brimful of energy.

'You sit with Teddy and rest,' Lex bade her, and Joy turned meekly back to the settee where Teddy was already dozing off his meal.

'Aren't you feeling well?' Margaret followed her back into the sitting room and looked at her anxiously. Perhaps worry over Lex and Dom had upset her. Anger at the geologist's reckless action boiled inside her. Did he not realise it affected others besides himself? she wondered wrathfully.

'I'm fine.' Joy smiled up at her, and this time the smile reached her eyes. Momentarily, they held a warm, happy glow. 'It's just that—well——' she hesitated shyly, 'it's early days yet,' she finished lamely.

'Do you mean . . . are you. . .?'

'She means that by next Christmas there'll be another little sock to hang up by the fireplace, besides Teddy's,' Sue cut across the confusion with a laugh. 'Or to be more accurate, a little bootee.'

'Oh, Joy, I'm so glad!' Margaret grasped her guest's slender hands joyfully. 'What lovely news. You are pleased, aren't you? You and Lex?' Joy's manner still held a hint of strain.

'We're both delighted,' Joy assured her warmly. 'We want a family. Three, if we can manage it. It's just that things at the moment are so uncertain. Lex's job. . . . If anything does go wrong,' her lovely eyes became suddenly much too bright, 'we seem a long way from home, and our families,' she confessed wretchedly.

'I could slay Dom!' Margaret's indignation boiled over. 'Of all the reckless, selfish creatures!' she breathed furiously.

'Don't say that,' Joy urged. 'Dom and Lex are doing the right thing, I'm sure.'

'Have they got the drills working again?' Sue put in eagerly. 'They haven't said, and I haven't dared to ask. You could cut the air between them with a knife,' she finished ruefully.

'They've finished the repair work, and started drilling,' Joy answered her readily enough. 'They've even found traces of hydrocarbons, as Dom said they would.' So he had been right, after all, Margaret thought bitingly. 'But they still haven't got down to oil, and Lex has only agreed to drill so far. After that, if they haven't made a strike, he's made Dom promise to pull out, and take the consequences of their action. That's why they're so on edge with one another,' she sighed and then smiled. 'Don't look so upset,' she told Margaret gently, 'Lex wants this oil find as much as Dom, now. If they do find commercial sized reserves in the basin, it would mean we could settle down for a year or two and concentrate on raising our family. Now we've got the option to purchase the house we're in, it would be ideal,' she said wistfully. 'I'm keeping my fingers crossed as much as Lex and Dom, but,' she paused, and her eyes filled with tears, 'I'm so afraid for them,' she confessed. 'For all of us, if they don't find oil, after what they've done.'

'And yet you still uphold what they're doing, even though you're worried half out of your mind about the consequences? And at a time when you most need peace?' Margaret stared at her incredulously.

'Dom's never been wrong yet,' Joy defended her attitude.

'There's always a first time.' Margaret remained unimpressed. 'And whether he's right or wrong about his wretched wildcat well is quite irrelevant,' she dismissed the whole exploratory venture as a triviality. 'He's wrong to cause you worry at a time like this, and I intend to tell him so!'

She started resolutely in the direction of the kitchen,

unheeding Joy's protests, all her instinct and training up in arms to protect the mother-to-be.

'We've finished the washing up and put it all away,' Lex told her virtuously, when she came in, and rather sheepishly removed her apron from around his much larger waist.

'Then go and keep Joy company, while I make a pot of tea.' Margaret shooed him in the direction of his wife.

'What can I do now?' Bill asked helpfully.

'Look after Teddy,' she took him up on his offer instantly. 'He's just waking up and wanting someone to play with.' She sent the house surgeon after Lex.

'What about me?' Sue watched her disposal tactics with raised eyebrows.

'Go and look after Bill.' Margaret handed her a job she knew the other girl would not refuse.

'Do I have an assignment, too?' Dom asked her quietly as the door closed behind the willing Sue.

'Yes—no——' Now they were alone, she found it curiously difficult to begin. 'You mustn't carry on with this crazy scheme of yours,' she burst out at last. 'You're worrying Joy half out of her mind, and she can't stand it.'

'It's mostly because of Joy that Lex agreed to help me,' Dom cut evenly across her tirade. 'And believe me. Joy can stand a lot more than what amounts to only a temporary anxiety, after all.' He was still so sure of himself, she thought, so certain that he must be in the right. 'Joy's got that sort of courage,' he said, and there was a wealth of respect and affection in his voice for the Jamaican girl.

For a moment Margaret knew a flash of envy. She would give everything she owned to be able to bring that tone to Dom's voice, that look to his eyes....

'She'll need her courage now for another purpose,' she pursued her point stubbornly.

'I'm aware of that.'

'You know Joy is...?'

'Expecting a baby? Yes,' he answered her calmly.

She had not expected him to know. She had thought to

thrust the knowledge at him, confounding him into agreeing to abandon his reckless defiance of his Board's orders, and now he had turned the tables, confounding her.

'You've got no right. . . .' she began hotly.

'Neither have you.' His voice hardened, and he slid to his feet from where he had been lounging nonchalantly on the edge of the table top. Margaret was reminded irresistibly of the fluid movements of a cat, rousing itself to spring. A wildcat? She backstepped hastily as he came close in front of her, and found herself up against the hard edge of the kitchen cupboard.

'Neither have you.' He pursued his advantage, and ruthlessly pinned her between himself and the wooden working surface.

'As a doctor. . . .' she began, desperately trying to don her armour.

'You're not Joy's doctor,' he disarmed her skilfully.

'We're friends,' she threw back defensively.

'When it comes to friendship, I've got the advantage of you.' His voice changed again, became lightly amused. 'I've known them longer, and closer.'

He had the advantage of her in more ways than one. She cast a quick glance to each side of her. Behind was the cupboard, on one side of her, the wall, and on the other, a heavy wing chair which resided in the kichen for the simple reason that she had nowhere else to put it. And Dom stood in front of her, apparently with not the slightest intention of moving. Her eyes flashed.

'Let me out.' Her voice was ominously quiet.

'Only if you pay a forfeit.' He made no attempt to hide his amusement now. 'It's a Christmas party, remember?' he derided her helplessness.

'I'll call the others.'

'You've just gone to a lot of trouble to send them away,' he reminded her, 'and like nicely behaved guests they've taken the hint and gone.'

'Oh, do stand aside and let me out,' she burst out. 'I

came in here to make a cup of tea. They'll wonder where it's got to.'

'It won't take long to boil a kettle, once you've paid your forfeit.' He was beginning to sound like a gramophone record with the needle stuck, she thought, her temper rising.

'It isn't Christmas, it's March,' she snapped. Why on earth had she ever suggested a Christmas party in the first place? She felt furious with herself, as much as with Dom.

'In that case, for something that must have been up there for three months, it's stayed remarkably fresh,' Dom commented, and raised his eyes interestedly to the ceiling beam above their heads. Automatically Margaret's eyes followed his gaze.

'Mistletoe? How did that get there?' She felt scarlet colour run up her throat and across her cheeks. 'I didn't put it there,' she denied hastily, before he could accuse her. He must not be allowed to think she had put it there, deliberately, hoping. . . .

'I didn't put it there,' she repeated desperately. Now she was beginning to sound like a gramophone record with the needle stuck, she thought hysterically.

'I didn't suggest you had,' he drawled lazily, 'but it seems a pity to waste it, now it's there.'

Margaret's face was still upturned towards the offending twigs, and it presented a perfect target. Dom's lips covered hers with practised precision. They stifled her protest, while his arms held her still, drawing her close against him in an enveloping embrace that denied her movement, while the mistletoe—whoever put it there—worked its age old magic above them. Caution stood no chance against its charms. The arguments that seemed so logical when she was not in Dom's arms faded and disappeared now he held her. Strong brown fingers caressing her fiery curls brushed away all desire to listen to arguments, however logical, and the feel of firm lips parting her own destroyed her will to withdraw.

'I love you,' were the only words her lips would form when at last he released them for a moment to press gentle kisses on her lowered eyelids, closing them to a dream of ecstasy that only the magic circle of his arms could hold.

'Dom—Dom——' she breathed his name.

'Where do you keep your cups, Maggie? Teddy wants a drink of pop.'

The door opened, and Bill Quinn stood there.

'Gosh, sorry,' he apologised. 'Shall I go out again, and knock before I come in?' he grinned, looking not in the least repentant at his untimely entrance.

'You could just go out again, and stay there,' Dom suggested, 'but I suppose if Teddy wants a drink. . . .' He conceded the house surgeon entry, and Margaret grabbed the kettle and turned hastily towards the taps, hiding her burning cheeks.

'I'm glad to see you've made use of Sue's bit of mistletoe,' Bill grinned irrepressibly. 'She thought it might come in handy some time during the party.'

'So now we know who put it there.' Dom slanted a look at Margaret, which she did her best to ignore. 'That's one question answered, at least,' he added quietly.

What did it matter who tacked up the piece of mistletoe? she wondered wretchedly. The question that tormented her mind had nothing to do with mistletoe—or with oil, for that matter.

'I love you!' Her lips—her heart—had admitted as much to Dom. If Bill had not come in when he did, would Dom have said the same to her? Once more the question returned to taunt her. This time she had not withdrawn from him, he would have had every opportunity to tell her, if he wanted to—if it had not been for Bill.

But did he want to? Or had the house surgeon's ill-timed entry been, for Dom, a welcome interruption?

CHAPTER FIFTEEN

PERHAPS even now, she might find out if Bill left them alone. It would only need a moment. . . . She lit the gas, and sorted out a brightly coloured mug from the cupboard.

'Joy said to give him only a drop,' Bill reported dutifully.

'That's all he's going to get. And it's not pop.' She partly filled the mug with fresh orange juice and handed it to the house surgeon. 'Give him that,' she began, when Bill interrupted.

'I don't think he trusts me to carry it. He's come to collect it for himself,' as the little boy toddled through the door with an enquiring look, and took the proffered mug with every evidence of satisfaction.

'Nice,' he pronounced, then, ' 'Nuff,' and handed her back the empty mug.

'It must have been to his liking,' Bill congratulated her.

'Wait a minute, not so fast!' Margaret scooped up the baby in her arms and sponged his face. 'Now you can go.' She set him on his feet again. And take Bill with you, she begged silently.

But Teddy was much too young to understand that grown-ups have their needs as well. He staggered to a halt in front of Dom and held up a pair of chubby arms.

'Carry,' he demanded, and the geologist reached down obediently and lifted him high into his arms.

'It looks as if I've found an assignment after all,' he said drily, and sent Margaret an oblique look across the child's head.

'I'll make the tea, and follow you in.' This time she welcomed the strident interruption of the kettle. It enabled her to turn away from Dom, to avoid his look by reaching into the cupboard for the tea caddy and cups, and when she turned back to deal with the kettle he was gone, and there was only Bill left with her in the kitchen. Silently the house surgeon helped her to set out two trays, his face unusually thoughtful as he went about his task.

'You carry this one in, and I'll take the one with the teapot on it.' He picked up the heavier tray, and stopped at the kitchen door with his foot propping it wide for Margaret to precede him.

'Be kind to him, Maggie,' he said unexpectedly, and she looked up at him, startled, but before she could find her voice to ask him what he meant he let the door swing to, and was already on his way to the sitting room door to repeat the performance for her benefit.

Be kind....

Dom said she was cruel. But it was Dom who was being cruel to her, not the other way round, her heart protested bitterly. He had played with her, roused her love and given nothing in return, keeping her on a rack of uncertainty over the meaning behind his actions, when there was probably no meaning at all. She ducked under Bill's arm into the sitting room, put her tray down on the small table which Lex thoughtfully dragged out for her, and summoned up a bright smile.

'Did Sue show you my tapestries?' She noticed with relief that Joy looked her usual bonny self again. 'I left some of them out for you to see.'

'They're lovely,' Joy enthused. 'And the chairs.' She stroked the tapestry-worked seat of the one nearest to her.

'Our Maggie's quite an accomplished needlewoman,' Bill remarked with a proprietorial air as he wielded the teapot for her.

'I'm not up to Joy's standard,' Margaret demurred, 'and don't call me Maggie,' she scolded automatically.

'It's a sign of affection,' Bill assured her solemnly. 'So long as I don't forget, and call you Maggie while we're on the wards,' he handed her a filled cup. 'I daren't, anyhow, not while you're wearing your white coat,' he confessed with a grin.

While she was wearing her armour. . . .

Bill's armour had frightened Teddy. 'It scared him off,' Dom said. But he had looked straight at Margaret when he said it. As if drawn by a magnet, her eyes found his, and in them she read the same unspoken accusation as before.

'Have you finally decided on the colours for your pair of tapestries?' With an effort she dragged her eyes away from the geologist, using Joy's needlework as an escape route.

'I'm still undecided about the wools for the shingle.' Fortunately Joy responded straight away. 'There's only a bit of it showing in the picture, but it's got to be just right. I hoped we might find time for a walk on the beach while we're here, then you could help me sort out the right shades,' she said. 'I brought the bundle of wools along, on the offchance.'

'If you're sure you feel up to it?' Margaret's heart leapt. A walk on the beach would give Dom an ideal opportunity to speak to her in privacy. They were bound to pair off.

'I'm perfectly all right,' Joy said happily, 'it's only really first thing, it wears off as the day goes on.'

Margaret found her heart racing as she shrugged into her coat and helped zip Teddy into a minute jump suit. The expanse of tide-washed shingle had never seemed so attractive to her before. But when they reached the beach, Lex suddenly became a solicitous husband, and insisted that Joy keep to the edge where it was easier to walk.

'It's bumpy where the stones have been tipped back after the storm. The tide hasn't had time to properly level them out again yet, and if you slip. . . .'

It was quite true. Margaret could still see the hillock that had blocked her own front door, and it had been joined by several larger hillocks tipped by the Council lorries which cleared the coast road. But if Joy kept to the edge of the beach, as hostess Margaret could not very well leave her on her own. Her heart sank.

'I think I'll keep to the edge as well,' Sue decided, 'I've got high heels on.'

They all seemed determined to foil her plans, and a childish lump of disappointment blocked her throat as Lex said,

'We'll take Teddy down to the water's edge,' in response to a series of urgent burbles and telegraphic arm wavings that left no doubt where the toddler wanted to go.

'Give me your other hand, then.' Dom reached down as Lex took hold of his son on the one side. 'We'll swing you over the rough bits.'

If his prompt reaction was any guide, it was a treat the baby was used to, and he did not wait for the first rough patch before they heard his high-pitched voice demanding, 'Swing!' Bill gave Sue a yearning look, but she shook her head firmly and pointed down towards her shoes.

'In that case, I'll join Lex and Dom, in case their arms get tired.' Bill wandered off after the other men, looking disconsolate. If only Dom had shown the same reluctance! With an effort, Margaret dragged her mind back to what Joy was saying.

'I'm glad I brought these wools along with me,' her guest held out the bundle of small skeins for the others to see. 'This one grey seems much too dark.'

'It is for this time of day.' Sue looked at it critically. 'If it was an early morning or evening scene, it would be just right.'

'Broad daylight for me,' Joy declared, 'with lots of sunshine stitched into the picture. That way, even if it's a bad day you've got some brightness captured on your wall.'

'There speaks someone who was born to sunshine,' Sue said enviously. 'But at least the days are beginning to lengthen. I thought this winter would never end, especially when that storm lasted for so long. But it's still light, and it's after half-past three,' she consulted her watch with satisfaction.

Instinctively Margaret glanced at her wrist to confirm

the time, and her forehead creased in a frown. On this score at least she was in no doubt of Dom's cruelty. He seemed to derive a sadistic pleasure in denying her the return of her watch.

'It's going cold. Shall we turn back?' she suggested. Suddenly she was tired of the walk, and wished she could go home alone and give way to the tears that threatened each time her mind dwelt on Dom—her watch——

'Oh, what a muddle it all is!' she exclaimed, her pent-up feelings refusing to be contained any longer.

'Cheer up, it'll sort itself out.' It was Joy's turn to act as comforter now. Mercifully she misinterpreted Margaret's meaning. Her mind ran on the oil rig and its future, while Margaret's ran on Dom, and her own. Joy slipped her hand through Margaret's arm. 'We shall know one way or another, very soon,' she consoled. 'At least, within the next few days, and by that time they'll either have found oil or not, either way they'll know what to do.'

If only her own problem was so clear cut! She tried to concentrate on the difficulties on the oil rig, but it gave her no comfort. If the well was sealed and abandoned. Dom would move on.

Setting the tea table when they returned to the cottage provided a welcome diversion, although it provided little relief from the strain.

'We should have kept Lex and Dom with us,' Joy observed, commenting on the heightened tension that was noticeable between the two men immediately they came back from the water's edge. 'They've been talking shop while they were away from us, though they promised not to.'

'Arguing shop would be more accurate,' Bill confirmed. 'They'd even got me taking sides,' he added gloomily.

'Which side?' Sue's voice held a warning.

'Both at once,' Bill grinned. 'I ended up by being a realist and an optimist, all at the same time.'

'They'd hoped for a progress report during the day.'

Joy's forehead puckered. 'They left your phone number with the rig, just in case. I hope you don't mind?'

'Of course not.' Margaret was as eager for news as the men.

'Their opposite numbers on the rig said they'd ring through right away, if there was any good news.'

The silence meant there was not. 'You did say it might be a day or two,' Margaret grasped at what comfort she could.

In fact, they had only just finished tea when the call came.

It was a tense meal. If it had not been for the presence of the child, it would have been an impossible one. Instinctively they all turned to Teddy for relief. His bright-faced delight at the simple red jelly and iced sponge with the cherries on top warmed away at least some of the strain from the faces of the adults around him. Even Sue and Bill looked troubled, although the fate of the oil rig did not directly affect them.

'Let's put a candle on the cake,' Sue suggested with desperate brightness after they finished eating. 'Look, he wants it lit again,' as Teddy's demanding wriggles and puffs provided a further welcome diversion.

'I'll do it for you.' Dom produced his lighter and an indulgent smile, and the small red Christmas candle glowed for the second time.

'One, two, three—blow!'

The miniature flame flickered and died, and with its going a silence fell upon the grown-ups. The game of gay pretence was over, extinguished with the candle flame, and stark reality lay between them like a shadow across the brightly decorated table, pregnant with unspoken thoughts.

The telephone bell shrilled loudly across the silence.

'I'll get it.' Lex jumped to his feet, nearly tripping over his chair in his haste.

'Lex, it's Margaret's phone. It might be for her,' Joy made an effort to restrain her husband.

'Go ahead,' Margaret gave her instant permission. 'If it turns out to be for me, you can always come back.'

But when he came back he shook his head, and his face was grave.

'It was for me,' he confirmed, and turned to Dom. 'We're wanted back on the rig, right away.'

'Did they say why?' The geologist's voice was quiet, tightly controlled, and Margaret's heart cried out to him. 'Don't shut me out. Let me help!' But he did not turn to look at her. His gaze was fixed unwaveringly on the drilling engineer. His face revealed nothing. In his expression was no sign of emotion, his eyes were blank and steely hard, but a muscle twitched spasmodically at the point of his jaw, betraying the intense strain he laboured under.

'No, but we've got no time to lose. The helicopter's on its way to collect us now.' Lex turned to Margaret. 'I'm sorry, it would happen on the day of your party,' he apologised.

'There'll be other parties. Don't worry, just go, and find out what they want of you.' She waved aside his apologies. Dom did not say he was sorry. He just looked at her, without speaking. His back was to the light, his eyes shadowed, their expression unfathomable. Her heart lurched as she met them, and her hands rose to her throat. Then he turned and followed Lex from the room as Bill said,

'I'll run Joy and Teddy home for you, when they're ready to go.'

'Thanks,' Lex accepted gratefully. 'We'll let you know how things progress.'

The door shut on his promise, and left behind a vacuum of doubt and uncertainty. Joy spoke into it, and even her soft voice seemed unaccountably loud in the silence.

'I think we're ready to go now, Teddy's dropped off to sleep.'

'It's been a full day. Don't wake him, I'll carry him for you.' Bill reached out and Joy surrendered the limp toddler into his arms.

'Don't disturb him to get dressed, I'll warm a travel rug to wrap him in.' Once more Teddy unwittingly provided a welcome diversion.

'We'll get these things cleared away, and leave you with a tidy house,' said Sue when they waved the others off, although Margaret would much rather they left the table as it was. The chore of clearing it would have given her something to occupy herself with when Bill eventually returned and took Sue away.

'It's been a lovely party, Maggie,' he thanked her with obvious sincerity. 'When Lex and Dom come back, we'll have another one to celebrate,' he tried to cheer her up, even though his own doubts showed clear in his face.

When would they come back? Margaret wondered drearily. And when they did, would it be good news they bore with them? She shared Bill's doubts. She knelt on the window seat, ignoring the late hour. She knew she would not sleep, so it was pointless going to bed. She strained her eyes through the darkness, trying to visualise what they would be doing on the rig. Why they had been sent for so suddenly. Perhaps they were having to do even more repairs, struggling against time, and hopeless odds.

It was useless to look out to sea, the rig was too far away to be visible from the shore, but perhaps, if she kept vigil at the window, she might catch a glimpse of the helicopter. She tilted her head back, searching the darkened sky, seeking a link, however tenuous, with Dom. But the sky remained as empty as the sea—as empty as her heart.

She awoke cramped, and stiff, and numb with cold. A rattle sounded from somewhere in the region of the front door. Her sleep-bemused mind located the direction of the sound, and she called out urgently,

'Dom! Don't go away. Dom....' It must be Dom, called to tell her his news. If she did not hurry he would go away again, thinking she was still asleep. 'Dom!' She stumbled to her feet and nearly fell, her cramped legs refusing for the moment to hold her. Desperately she forced her frozen limbs to carry her through the hall to the front door. With urgent fingers she fumbled at the bolt, and managed to swing it inwards. The blast of cold air that came through the opening shocked her into full wakefulness, and she stared at the cheery face of the newspaper delivery boy confronting her from the porch outside.

''Morning, doctor.' He held out his delivery towards her. 'I can't get your monthly mag through the letter box this morning. It's got a supplement in it, or something, and it's made it too thick.'

His effort to force it through the letter box must have been the rattle she heard. She took the morning newspaper and her magazine from his hands, heard her own voice thank him, and he went off on his bicycle, whistling. And except for the boy, there was no one on the frontage of the cottages. No sports car. No Dom. . . .

Margaret forced herself to drink a cup of coffee and eat something, she could not afterwards remember what. It was Monday morning, and she would need all her energy to cope with the day. She told herself aloud what day it was, so that she would not forget. There were ward rounds to do, patients to attend to, the first clinic of the week to take. She needed to be busy, but with the perversity of fate the day turned out to be an unusually quiet one, uneventful, with nothing of sufficient importance to demand her entire concentration, to occupy her mind to the exclusion of Dom.

'That's the lot for today, Doctor.' Sister took up the case records in her capable arms. 'We can close on time for once.'

'No more patients waiting?'

'Nary a one.' Sister bustled off with her burden of paperwork, and Margaret unbuttoned her white coat with a sigh.

'I was wrong, there is one more.' Sister stuck her head back through the door. 'Go on through,' Margaret heard her speak to someone in the corridor beyond. 'Doctor's free.

She's finished for the day.' It was an odd thing for her to say, and surprisingly Sister did not return with the last comer as she would normally have done. Instead, she closed the door behind her with a firm click, and disappeared. Margaret turned, and looked up.

'What can I do for you?' she began, then stopped. Stared.

'Dom!'

She did not immediately recognise him. It took a few seconds for the fact to register that the tall figure in steel-capped boots and oil-stained boiler suit, with an orange tin helmet set at a jaunty angle on his pale hair, was the geologist. Her eyes flew to his face. It was darkly streaked with oil, inadequately wiped clean with a hasty hand. Perhaps they had had to do some more repairs, after all. But his eyes were as blue as ever, and they smiled at her, and his lips smiled too, inviting her. She did not allow herself to think, this time. She whirled towards him, and he took one swift stride, closing the distance between them. Suddenly she was in his arms, and all the doubts and fears and uncertainties vanished as if they had never been.

'I'm oily.'

'I don't care!'

To prove it, she kissed the streak across his face. The moment her lips touched his cheek he turned his head and covered them with his own, urgently, thirstily, draining their sweetness like a parched desert traveller drinks deeply at a life giving pool.

'My love, my heart. . . .' he whispered.

Could it really be Dom, who murmured endearments like purest poetry as his lips left her own at last, and pressed ruffled gold curls against her ear; touched the delicate blue veins of her temples, and returned again to her lips as if, no matter how much he drank, life itself could not be long enough to assuage his thirst.

'I was so afraid I'd lose you.' His voice was hoarse with longing as he released her at last, and drew her down to sit beside him on the brightly coloured clinic bench.

'Lose me?' She did not understand. How could he lose her, when he owned her heart?

'With my career at stake, I had no right. . . .' He stopped, and for a moment his eyes lost their smile and became bleak. 'But it's different now.'

'Tell me?'

'I've made your coat oily,' he noticed with concern.

'It doesn't matter.' It didn't, any more. She would never need to wear it as an armour against him again. 'Have you had to do some more repair work?' She stroked a gentle forefinger across the smudge on his cheek.

'Not repair work. That isn't engine oil splashed all over me. It's raw crude, straight from under the sea,' he told her exultantly.

'You've found the deposits you were looking for? You were right, after all!' Her eyes glowed, glorying in his rightness.

'Did you ever doubt it?' he asked her, mock severely.

'Never!' All she ever doubted was his love, and now he had laid that doubt to rest. He could have done so a long time ago, but she respected his male need to offer her security. The pain of waiting no longer mattered.

'I didn't stop to change, I had to tell you right away. There's all the evidence of a big find in the basin.' His eyes shone with enthusiasm.

'What Lex calls a commercial find?' The jargon rose naturally to her lips, as excitement rose within her, matching his. 'Your wildcat well was justified, after all?'

'It isn't a wildcat any more,' he smiled down at her. 'It's been tamed. We'll be spudding in a production well on the site, there's oil and gas in large quantities, just as I knew there would be.'

'We must let Joy know. She'll be so glad, they'll be able to buy their house and settle down, just as they wanted to.'

'Lex is on his way to tell her now. He dropped me at the shop at the top of the High Street.'

'The paper shop?' They didn't want any more balloons, the party was over.

'No, the shop next to it,' he answered mysteriously.

'That's a jewellers.' What did he want at a jewellers?

'I went to retrieve this for you,' he explained, smiling. 'Let me put it back where it belongs.'

'My watch?' Margaret gasped her delight as he slipped the familiar bracelet round her wrist. 'But you said it was treasure trove. . . .'

'You treasured it. That was enough for me,' he told her gravely. 'I had to make sure its ducking hadn't done any damage, before I returned it to you. And I've had the bracelet fixed too, so it won't slip off your wrist again.'

She thanked him sweetly, without words, and when some time later she nestled happily against him, safe at last in the circle of his arms, he went on softly,

'While I was at the jewellers, they told me this was ready, too.' Strangely, for once he seemed unsure of himself, oddly diffident, and Margaret raised her eyes to his face enquiringly. It seemed so unlike the confident Dom she knew. 'I had it made a while ago, hoping. . . .' He broke off, and showed her the contents of the red leather ring box that lay in his palm.

'It's beautiful!' she breathed. A solitaire diamond winked from the centre of a gold heart, its clear pure fire reflecting the fire of passion in his eyes.

'That's where you'll always be—right in the middle of my heart.' He slipped the ring on her engagement finger and drew her to him hungrily. 'I love you—I love you.' With urgent lips he sought to convince her. 'Marry me, Maggie,' he begged, using her nickname for the first time.

She nodded happily. She could not speak, because the ardour of his kisses did not leave her lips free to form the words, but her nod seemed to tell him all he wanted to know. His voice calling her Maggie sounded like sweetest music in her ears, and when at last she lay back in his arms, it was with confidence enough to tease.

'I thought you didn't want encumbrances,' she murmured wickedly.

'You won't be an encumbrance. You'll be my wife.'

And that sounded sweeter still.

Harlequin Romances

The books that let you escape
into the wonderful world of romance!
Trips to exotic places...interesting
plots...meeting memorable people...
the excitement of love....These are
integral parts of Harlequin Romances—
the heartwarming novels read by
women everywhere.

Many early issues are now available.
Choose from this great selection!

Choose from this list of Harlequin Romance editions.*

ome of these book were originally published under different titles.

Relive a great love story...
Harlequin Romances 1980
Complete and mail this coupon today!

Harlequin Reader Service

In U.S.A.
MPO Box 707
Niagara Falls, N.Y. 14302

In Canada
649 Ontario St.
Stratford, Ontario, N5A 6W2

Please send me the following Harlequin Romance novels. I am enclosing my check or money order for $1.25 for each novel ordered, plus 59¢ to cover postage and handling.

☐ 422	☐ 509	☐ 636	☐ 729	☐ 810	☐ 902
☐ 434	☐ 517	☐ 673	☐ 737	☐ 815	☐ 903
☐ 459	☐ 535	☐ 683	☐ 746	☐ 838	☐ 909
☐ 481	☐ 559	☐ 684	☐ 748	☐ 872	☐ 920
☐ 492	☐ 583	☐ 713	☐ 798	☐ 878	☐ 927
☐ 508	☐ 634	☐ 714	☐ 799	☐ 888	☐ 941

Number of novels checked @ $1.25 each = $_____

N.Y. State residents add appropriate sales tax $_____

Postage and handling $_____ .59

TOTAL $_____

I enclose _____
(Please send check or money order. We cannot be responsible for cash sent through the mail.)

Prices subject to change without notice.

NAME _____
(Please Print)

ADDRESS _____

CITY _____

STATE/PROV. _____

ZIP/POSTAL CODE _____

Offer expires May 31, 1981   01156337